# LUNA JOYA

# HOW TO
# DATE
# A FURY

## SYN CITY SHIFTERS
### ❧ BOOK ONE ❧

MYSTIC OWL

AN IMPRINT OF CITY OWL PRESS

# HOW TO DATE A FURY

LUNA JOYA

MYSTIC OWL

HOW TO DATE A FURY
San City Shifters, Book 1

MYSTIC OWL
A City Owl Press Imprint
www.cityowlpress.com

Cover Design by MiblArt. All stock photos licensed appropriately.

Edited by Lisa Green.

For information on subsidiary rights, please contact the publisher at info@cityowlpress.com.

Print Edition ISBN: 978-1-64898-237-8

Digital Edition ISBN: 978-1-64898-238-5

Printed in the United States of America

# ALSO BY LUNA JOYA

**The Legacy:**

*Tides of Time (Prequel)*

*Magic Touch*

*Killing Song*

*Heart and Seek*

*Flash Point*

\*\*\*

**The Wicked:**

*Wicked Crown*

*Wicked Match*

*Wicked Grace (Coming 2023)*

# PRAISE FOR THE WORKS OF LUNA JOYA

"A witch and an FBI agent find love while solving a years-old murder in the wickedly delightful second paranormal romance in Joya's *Legacy* series. The anticipation is delicious, and the eventual romance is well worth the wait. This sexy love story will entice longtime paranormal fans and draw in new readers." — *Publishers Weekly*

"Passionate and heartfelt, *Wicked Crown* delivers! Step into the goblin realm where court intrigue mixes with page-turning plot, Joya's electric foray into fantasy romance." — *J.E. McDonald, author of the Wickwood Chronicles*

"A magical debut full of unique, complex characters, fabulous sisterhood and an adorable dog. Who could ask for anything more?" — *Felicia Grossman, Historical Romance Author*

"With fast paced, heart pounding, thrilling suspense and fantastic displays of supernatural powers, *Magic Touch* is a paranormal delight! The romance isn't anything to sneeze at either! There is romance echoing through time and scorching the present. Readers will feel the heat of instant attraction and the sorcery of levitating passions." – *InD'tale*

"*Tides of Time* was one of those reads that kept my hands locked around my e-reader and my butt firmly planted in my chair. This book promises witchy mystery and romance, and it doesn't disappoint." — *Evie Drae, author of Queer Romance*

"A HOT romance with excellent chemistry between the characters, and a paranormal aspect that was both intriguing and contained a unique spin on magical powers." — *Amber K. Bryant, Award-Winning Author*

"Highly enjoyable. I was engaged from beginning to end. I was delighted in the different ways the author chose to incorporate magic into the book. These characters were well written. I hope to read more about these witchy sisters! I loved the chemistry between Cami and Sam. A wonderful debut for Luna Joya." — *The Literary Vixen*

"*Killing Song* is the high-octane third paranormal romance in Joya's *Legacy* series. Joya holds the reader in her grip with action-packed intrigue and an expertly paced will-they-or-won't-they. The satisfying ending still leaves plenty of room for the series to continue; readers will be eager to see that it does." — *Publisher's Weekly*

"*Heart and Seek* is a powerhouse of political intrigue, magical secrets, and sexy characters... For readers who love witches flexing their magical muscle, who drool over an intricate plot, and who believe that a love match should always prevail over a power match – this is it! This is a fabulous read. What will the delightfully devious Luna Joya bring us next?" — *InD'tale*

"Joya sends out her *Legacy* series with an enticing fifth paranormal romance, *Flash Point,* that finds the five Donovan sisters working to defeat the demon Nymvyra once and for all. The emotional friends-to-lovers romance plays out as a tanta-lizing tug-of-war between Mina and Josh, while the multilayered suspense plot provides satisfying answers to series-long questions. Readers are sure to be pleased." — *Publisher's Weekly*

*For Katherine, a true roller derby queen*

# 1

## DOTTIE

Momma always warned me that coming to Syn City would be the death of me, but taking my first step into The Rink tonight, I've never felt so alive.

A massive indoor coliseum with seats stretching to the tippy top, the place vibrates with excitement. Thrumming bass pours through the speakers. The cold air conditioning blasts my sweaty skin, chasing away the hot, sticky humidity of the summer night. I'm a grown woman who had to sneak past her mother to make it here, but like a kid in a sweet shop, I gape at the oval-shaped skating track below that's the center stage.

A woman struts to the middle of the rink. "Welcome beloved humans," she booms into a bedazzled microphone. "You've come to see the seven Houses, yes?" The way she asks the question invites only one answer. Piercing whistles, thundering applause, and rowdy yells echo from every direction.

Shuffling forward with the other humans in line, I'm on sensory overload, trying to memorize the sights, sounds, and smells so I can tell Connie every detail when a woman wearing a neon shirt that says *Naughty* waves me forward. Her hair shimmers iridescent blue streaked with green. Those sparkling strands could be a trick of the light, but I'm guessing they mark her as supernatural.

"Your ticket?" she asks.

My cheeks heat, and my heart bangs a *here-stands-a-newb* gong beat. "I showed it at the door. Didn't know I'd need it again." My voice comes out too high. *Great.* Now, everyone knows I'm a Rink virgin. Shoving my hand into my pocket, I fish for the wadded mess.

"You'll want to find your seat before the show starts unless you scored pit passes." She tips her head toward where the announcer stands.

"No. I'm not in the pit tonight." As if I could ever be. Anyone with an eye or two or three could tell that I can't afford to buy my way into the pit and don't have the gods-loved luck to win my way in. My cousin Connie teases I was born with enormous luck, all of it bad. Fifteen to my ancient twenty-four, Connie knows everything. Just ask her.

"All right then." The woman's sugar-sweet voice coats the innocent statement with raw sexual insinuation that has me blushing again. She must be a Nymph. I should've known which of the seven Houses she came from with her perfect hair, figure, and face. "Let's see what seat you've picked."

I pull out the wadded ticket and try to smooth it. My efforts do nothing except smear the ink. "Sorry."

The Nymph glances at the wrinkled mess. "Ah, the nosebleed section. You're wanting the highest viewpoint for your first trip?"

"Yes." That explanation sounds much better than I counted my coins ten times when figuring out how much the ticket and trip would cost. I didn't have the money to take the air-conditioned hover ferry that brought most people here. No, I'd ridden the hot and cramped bus across the bridge that spans the massive lake inhabited by sea hags and water creatures waiting to snatch crash victims into the depths. But I'm not discussing my sad cleaning lady pay with the daughter of a goddess. "I've always wanted to see the show." It's the truth, something I don't get to say at home.

"Of course, who doesn't? It's the grandest event in the world. Your name?" A musical lilt to her voice draws me in.

I shouldn't give her my true name, shouldn't give anyone here any information about me according to the horror stories my momma has spun. But tonight's about taking chances, going on new adventures before I'm permanently stuck in my tiny hometown. "Dottie."

"Dorothy?" she asks.

"Nope, just plain Dottie." Because momma said I was a plain-looking baby from the start. No way I'd be sharing that pitiful detail with the Nymph, hypnotic voice or not. Even my cousin Connie can claim Constance with a long list of middle names, but then she might rather have a living mother, I suppose.

"Okay, not-at-all plain Dottie, this way." The Nymph strolls through the crowds toward the far side of the coliseum, waving her hand at the booths set up along the back wall at this level. "So you don't miss a moment once the show starts, we have the concessions, merchandise, and signing booths here on the mezzanine." The longest line snakes from where one of the players chats prettily and signs photos, caps, and body parts.

"A Muse?" I ask. Definitely not a Gorgon with those striking looks, and probably not a Styx since the woman signing doesn't give off an undead vibe and she's unmasked, but she could be a Huntress maybe. Or a Mad Mae. She smiles too much to be a Fury. I wouldn't remember all seven Houses except their banners stand like silent soldiers surrounding the rink. "Or a Nymph?" She doesn't have my guide's blue hair and sparkle, but she'd lure enough suitors to her table to keep her busy for hours.

"Ugh, no way she'd be a member of my House." The Nymph sounds annoyed I might've considered such a notion. "Fancy-ass Muses might have talent, but they don't have our skills in the sack."

All right, lesson learned. Don't confuse the Houses. Most certainly don't mix up Muses with Nymphs. Probably best to skip the guessing in the future. "What else is on this level?"

"The magical makeup booths, although they're not really magic, you know, just tech. And the most important place in The Rink besides the rink itself—our bar."

Glancing at the ginormous bar with bright-colored liquor bottles lining the high shelves, I do a double take at the bartender with dark blond hair and tanned skin, prowling from customer to customer with a grace no man that size should possess. Seeing him sends me back to my fifteenth birthday. Not some happy party full of cake and candles and wishes coming true, but me waiting alone at the bus stop in the cold rain for a boy who never showed. Shaking off the memory, I hurry to catch the Nymph. No way would I let Chase Malone ruin another night for me. Not ever again.

The lights lower, and a hush falls over the crowd. Scents of popcorn and sugary treats waft from the concessions, and my belly grumbles, loud and obnoxious.

"Maybe you should stop for snacks before you climb to your seat," the Nymph suggests with a provocative giggle that softens the insult. Something tells me she takes little in life all that seriously, and I envy her for that.

"I skipped dinner. Excitement," I lie. Lack of cash is more like it.

"Don't pass out from hunger on us. The seven Houses guarantee safety here to our human visitors. You already look damaged enough." She glances at the scrapes on my legs and arms.

Oops, maybe my shorts and tank top show too much bruised skin, but it's roasting outside. Swamp and summer mean sweat. Being klutzy and a professional cleaner mean a rainbow of nicks and bangs color my skin. "It's nothing."

"Uh huh." Obviously not believing me, she points toward the

highest seats to our right. "You're up there at the top, halfway in. Grab something to eat, don't fall out on your way up, and enjoy the show. Word of advice: you can be *anything* in Syn City so decide what it is you really want or maybe *who* you will become while you're here. See you around, Dottie doll." With the good-bye, she spins, beautiful blue hair waving around her as if submerged in a storybook drawing, and leaves me by myself in this strange, supernatural city.

Doing the math, if I splurge on popcorn and a soda, I'll need to take the latest bus home. My stomach growls again as if deciding for me. I buy both, knowing I'll regret the wait later at the bus stop long after the crowds have gone home. Memories of that night waiting for Chase to show haunt me again, and I stomp up the stairs, leaving the ugly past behind one sticky step at a time.

"The seven Houses welcome you as our guests," the announcer booms. "You know the history, but we're here to remind you."

Beams of red illuminate the dark ceiling. Acrobats drop from the rafters on invisible strings with their glittery hoops and fluttering ribbons. They pause, hanging in suspended stillness and waiting for the story to continue as if actors in an aerial play.

The announcer raises her microphone, demanding the audience's full attention again. "Decades ago, the Witching Wars pitted neighbor against neighbor in the attempted genocide of those deemed *different*. The violence first erupted in that now great witch sanctuary, the City of Angels."

Women with elaborate black and silver wings dive fast and low from the ceiling. My breath catches, and my still starving belly swoops and slides into snarled knots, suddenly silent. Gasps and whispers come from below. *The Furies.* Connie had told me the rumors that some of them had real wings, but I'd thought it gossip spun to sell tickets. Seeing them fly in person? *Incredible.*

The announcer glances upward, cocking her hip to one side

as if annoyed that the women above stole her spotlight. "The humans burned witches and attempted to wipe out the supernaturals. For years, the two sides clashed in epic, awful battles."

Harlequin-masked dancers drop from the shadows, spreading ribbons that unfurl in red, yellow, and orange like flames. The Mad Maes, they had to be. If the silly masks weren't proof enough, those toy guns shooting "pow" signs would be. Their maniacal laughter sends shivers racing over my skin. Legends say those women could drive anyone insane. Of course, the tabloid Connie reads could've been lying, but who would want to test the theory? Not me. That's for sure. I have enough problems without pissing off some booze god's psycho daughters.

"Death reigned." This time the announcer pauses for undead beauties rising from the floor inside the pit. My heart *bump-da-dumps* faster in my chest, fear wrapping around the poor battered thing and squeezing. I walk into hazmat situations nightly with gross and disturbing discoveries, but the Styx weave dread through the room like a coven's super spell. I'd read descriptions of the women who wore faceless masks and were rumored to come from their namesake's river, but I hadn't believed the hype. Now I do.

The Rink's audience goes deathly silent, no pun intended. No one dares speak or whisper or even crunch on snacks. The announcer thumping the mic has me and others jumping in our seats. "When magic returned to the public realm, when humans realized that the powers were real, the old gods woke. They brought forth their mortal deity daughters, made in their divine essence." Running a hand along her curves, she shimmies and shakes to whistles and catcalls. "So now, you luckies have the seven Houses, their Syndicate, and Syn City, where everyone who's anyone comes to parrrrty." Her prolonged rebellious yell breaks the tension that has my shoulders creeping toward my ears.

She only told basic history. Everyone knows it, although

seeing the major milestones acted out so vividly makes me wonder if parts hadn't been left out of our human history books. But I don't think on the possibility long with the sudden glitz and glamour exploding throughout The Rink. Fireworks bang, and smoke fills the air, stinging my nose and eyes. Relief comes when waves of spice and sage roll through, clearing the path.

The Furies zoom to the rafters, cloaked in darkness, and a show begins that's part burlesque, part circus, part rock concert —all mixed and spun in a spectacular extravaganza. No holograms here. It's loud and live and all-consuming.

Singers and dancers transform the stage into oceans, clouds, and space in a frenzied, fever dream of flashing lights and thumping music. At some invisible signal, the performers stop, freezing in place. Our applause comes in a deafening cacophony of clapping hands and stomping feet. I'm swept into the excitement with everyone else. For a glorious moment, I'm part of a bigger, better whole.

Muses and Nymphs rush off stage with winks and blown kisses that project a thousand times larger than their already bigger-than-life presences on the holo-screens, covering the house banners with beautiful faces and graceful strength. I spot my earlier usher with her *Naughty* shirt in the prism of mermaid and unicorn-colored hair.

A spotlight pierces the sudden darkness, focusing on the announcer who has changed into a jewel-encrusted bodysuit. Rubies, sapphires, and diamonds wink when she raises the microphone. Real gems? Maybe. It's The Rink. Anything goes.

"Who enjoyed the pre-show?" she asks, pausing for us to lose our collective minds. "Ready for the real show?" Another pause, another surge of applause. "We have a roller derby bout—that's a game or match for our first-time visitors—for you tonight between last year's champions, the Huntresses, and their closest contender, the Furies." Cheers for both houses go up from the crowd. "You may have heard the rumor that the best player for the Furies has retired from the league?" She drawls out the last with fake sympathy, putting her manicured hand over her glittering chest. "It's true."

A collective groan comes from my right along with heckles from lower down the stands.

Like a giant middle finger to the announcer, or maybe the crowd, the Furies zip onto the rink, speeding along the flat track on tricked-out roller skates. With names like Slaya and Killa, the mortal daughters of vengeance deities dominate through punk rock badassery.

The holo-screens pick up tiny details of their uniforms that I otherwise couldn't see from so far away—fishnet tights, skull-printed laces, and wings on the backs of their jerseys. The Huntresses swarm the rink, but I can't take my eyes off the Furies. Their *look-at-us* ferocity doesn't have the same brutality as the Gorgons or the creep factor of the Styx, but it's amazing. So amazing that I feel bad for them when they lose, and I stay until the last Fury rolls off the rink.

I linger in the stands as long as I dare. Floodlights blare like sunlight blazing on the track, exposing some of its secrets. I can make out trap door seams along with a massive sunken section of the pit floor that must raise and lower, a giant platform to cast the illusion of performers appearing out of thin air.

At the bar, a grey-haired man scrubs and scours to loud rock music. I haven't cleaned restaurants and bars in years, other than crime scene cleanups. My gigs come from human law agencies or from the marshals who serve the shifters. Maybe Syn City doesn't have to sanitize as much since the belief you could catch lycanthropy from drinking after a shifter seems to be a thing of the past except in my puny hometown of Petunia. There's no sign of the handsome hottie who'd made me remember Chase.

My high school dream guy, Chase had gorgeous green eyes that seemed to take in everything except my galaxy-sized crush on him. Tall with broad shoulders and lean muscles, he'd been as coordinated as I am clumsy. The guy could literally drop off a ladder from defacing homecoming banners and land on his feet. I'd trip just looking at the same ladder. The cheerleaders had made fun of me for wearing hand-me-down threads, and Chase had wanted revenge on my behalf. It seems so petty now, but then? His standing up for me had meant everything. Until he actually stood me up.

Ugh, I shove aside the memory again. I haven't thought of him so much in years. Okay, okay, so I worried about what'd happened to him since his whole family had disappeared with him, and I wondered how things might've played out if that night had gone differently. Would I still be in Petunia, the small town full of big mouths? Would I be single? Would he mind the lingering scent of ammonia in my hair or the clunky, steel-toed boots required for my job? But his green eyes and lazy smile only came to mind once a day now instead of once an hour.

A man slams into me, or maybe I slam into him. The quick contact knocks me back to reality. "Oof." My breath rushes out, and I trip over my heavy boots, dreading the drop to the concrete floor.

He grabs for me, losing his grip on a big cardboard box that sends glittering balls bouncing in all directions with a perky *ping-ping-ping*. "Are you okay?"

*I did that.* My daydreaming about stuff best forgotten did that. "I am sooo sorry." Scrambling to my knees, I chase one ball, then another as the first slips from my fingers. "I should've been paying more attention to where I was going."

"No worries as long as you're all right." He crouches next to me, a skinny, baby-faced guy in his thirties in a long-sleeved shirt with *The Rink* printed across the front. "I didn't realize any guests were around, or I would've ducked through an inner corridor." He joins me in corralling the runaway balls.

The casual way he mentions my loitering has me cringing. "I'm on my way out to catch the late bus."

What I said has him snapping his head up, his gaze meeting mine. "Alone? Everyone has either caught the ferry or headed to the pleasure district. The bus stop will be deserted."

Anxiety crawls up my spine, but I push it away. Or I do a right fine job of ignoring it, at least. I'm too poor to afford worrying about stuff I can't change. "I'll be okay."

He looks unsure, then nods in a bobblehead bounce that reminds me of a bumbling imitation of the glitter balls around us. "Overthinking things is part of my job."

I catch myself grinning. It's nice to hear someone else second-guesses everything. "How so?"

"I'm the props manager here."

"For that pre-show?" Excitement bubbles through me like fizzy soap suds. "The flying Furies, the streamers and swords for the Mad Maes, the dancers and everything else? So amazing."

"Thanks. I do my best. Can you imagine if I misplaced a Styx's ceremonial cape or swapped out a Muse's microphone for a plain one without the sparkles?" He chuckles as if either might be a fate worse than death. "You human?"

"Yeah, is it so obvious?"

"Humans keep Syn City going. If visitors like you didn't bring in the money, the Houses couldn't afford the many useless toys I keep track of, such as hundreds of bouncing balls to amuse the Mad Maes." He stands at the same time I do, brushing his fingers against mine when he takes the last glittery ball from me. His touch is shy and sweet in an old-fashioned kind of way with no hint of a spark. I'm only attracted to blond-haired, green-eyed bad boys. Maybe it's a chronic affliction with a magical cure.

I clear my throat. "I'm afraid I don't bring in much cash for new toys, or I wouldn't be taking the late bus. I've always heard Syn City was completely safe, but I'll admit you've freaked me out a bit about the abandoned bus stop."

"No, no, the town's safe. Sorry about that. Want me to walk you out now that I've spooked you? I need to finish up here, but I should be done in time. Or I could ask security if you don't mind shifters."

Something about the last weirds me out. I've been cleaning up supernatural messes for years. Walking to a bus stop should be no big deal, and frankly, this guy looks no stronger than me. His arms and legs could double as twigs. In fact, I'm probably tougher after years of putting up with bullies and shoveling toxic dumps in Petunia. "I'll be fine, but thanks for the offer."

"No worries. Maybe see you around again?"

"Hopefully." My empty bank account disagrees.

"My name's Marty. Ask for me so I can get you a ticket discount."

"I'm Dottie, and thanks." What a nice guy.

"Least I can do to make up for running over you. Hope to see you again soon." He struggles to lift the box as though it weighs a million pounds and staggers away under the load. I'm glad I refused his gallant offer to walk me to the bus stop. The gear I heft on my cleaning jobs would outweigh his jumbo collection of bouncy glitter balls a hundred times over.

Sticky heat smacks me in the face as I step out of The Rink, clinging to my skin as though I'd somehow dared to betray the weather spirits by hiding in an air-conditioned oasis. Sweat droplets roll down my back, and my hair sticks to my cheeks. Summer nights don't get much cooler than the days here.

Along the path to the bus stop, vines and moss blanket the trees and bushes. The smell of swamp stench comes at me in violent waves as though the marsh might be reclaiming this city one inch at a time. Crickets and bullfrogs serenade me with their chirps and bellows. Water sloshes from not so far away. Thank the tech gods for the flickering lights that hover above, casting a blue and gold glow between the swallowing shadows.

I'm alone out here, far from the pounding music of the pleasure district's clubs and bars and whatever else. A tingling sensation wriggles down my neck, more than just another sweat bead spilling. The prickling has shivers dancing along my arms, more menacing than the Mad Maes. My heart kicks into overdrive, bumping harder than those distant beats.

Resisting the urge to run, I sneak a glance over my shoulder. Nothing there. *Stupid.* Except a rustling comes from somewhere nearby that's louder than the pounding pulse in my ears. Terror steals my breath, and I tear down the path, gravel sliding beneath my heavy boots. Years of running from bullies means I'm fast.

The sweat slicking my skin turns clammy. Fear flows like iced tea through my veins, and my throat closes thicker than molasses in January. I slip and stagger and screech louder than a barn owl.

*Syn City's a safe zone, protected by the Syndicate.* The thinking part of my brain fires the message on repeat, but the primal part —the instinct that knows monsters under the bed can be real— screams to run *faster.*

A crunch of gravel behind me has me spinning, fists clenched and feet ready to deliver an ass kicking in these boots. Not that I know how, but I'll face down whoever or whatever is coming for me. Momma might've raised me to smile through whatever nasty comes my way, but she didn't raise a coward. With a fighting yell, I glimpse a figure taller than me, a hooded sweatshirt, and a massive hammer coming at my head.

I hear the whir of speeding air.

Then...nothing.

## 2

---

# CHASE

I HAVEN'T SEEN DOTTIE NORTH OUTSIDE OF DREAMS OR WAKING fantasies in nine long years, not since I left her waiting for me at a bus stop. We'd been running away for her fifteenth birthday, coming here to Syn City to see the show. But the same full moon night, I'd killed my stepfather, which got me shipped out of town permanently. Probably for the best since sweet Dottie is human, and I'm not.

Still, I'd fooled myself that I'd caught her scent earlier tonight in The Rink. Then, I'd looked up from where I poured yet another pretentious drink for yet another rich tourist who'd come to slum it with the supernaturals and gape at the daughters of old deities. For a second, a pounding heartbeat, I'd seen her lanky, long-limbed, sun-kissed self with the same heart-shaped face and shiny hair. Her scent, fresh and teasing with a hint of her rose-perfumed shampoo had tickled my nose.

But the crowd had closed in, and when the masses parted again, my dream girl had been just that, a dream and nothing more. I wouldn't go chasing the impossible, not even to hear her call my name in her honeysuckle drawl one more time.

Yet, like a dumb dog, I'd followed a brown ponytail and the

same scent outside The Rink to the deserted path that leads to the bus stop. Moments ago, the rose perfume had turned sour, tinged with panic. Cat shifter senses on high alert, I scan the dirt and gravel path, the thick tree branches that lace overhead together like a spider's web. The floating glow lamps don't do much to light the path, but I can see better than most in the dark.

A short scream comes from far away, and my predator nature kicks in, scenting prey in flight. I hear a thud, and I move. Risking a full shift outdoors in Syn City without permission could get me exiled, but I don't need to shift in order to run fast and do serious damage, especially if the threat's a mere human. The metallic scent of antique coins comes on the wind. *Blood.* Someone's hurt —badly, judging by the strength of the smell.

"Dottie?" I yell her name, feeling like an idiot because what are the chances my high school crush has come to the place that her mother believed represented sin incarnate? To the place she'd sworn she wouldn't visit unless we came together? Of course, I'd broken my promise to her first.

Glancing over my shoulder, I judge the distance back to The Rink. Too far to wait for help, no matter how much the seven Houses want to be the first on any scene. Whoever has been hurt would have to settle for me instead.

Unsheathing my claws in a partial shift that's a perk of alpha bloodlines, I charge forward, rounding a corner where the smell of blood overpowers me. Something lumbers away downwind through the trees. A deer maybe? Or a coyote? Sea creatures haven't been spotted this far into land, and I don't have time to waste investigating.

Earlier, I'd hoped I'd spotted Dottie in The Rink.

Now, I hope to hell that I didn't.

A giant, winged creature blinks into the path in front of me, and I skid to a stop, kicking up gravel. Sure, several of the seven Houses can fly, not just the flashy shit they break out for the pre-show or the winged derby bouts reserved for supernatural VIP invites. But even the biggest Gorgons don't loom this large.

Checking my sudden need to run away from whatever this is, I stand my ground, claws out. I'm not packing away my best weapons until I figure out what's going on.

"Hello?" I ask, not impressing anyone, including myself, with my IQ tonight. Following a fantasy out into the swamp hadn't been smart, but what can I say? Being curious comes with being a cat. "You with the Houses? If not, you might want to take off."

She turns in super slow motion, and with my night vision, I can tell that she's a *she*—a ghastly, fuckin' terrifying *she* who wouldn't be my choice to cross on a dark path except here we both stand.

Dread wraps around me, spearing deep beneath my skin as though she's cracked the whip curled on her hip and squeezed all the air from my lungs. Her enormous black wings could be dragon wings if she'd been less upright, two-legged, and humanoid. Maybe they're bat wings? Or maybe I've spent too much time reading old-school comic books that escaped the burnings after the Witching Wars. Dark hair blows around her face as if the wings stir their own wind.

Wearing a short dress and thigh-high boots that might be scary sexy on anyone else, she's pale with black coils snaking around her arms, legs, and neck. Gods, let those be living, moving tattoos and not actual serpents. I hate snakes.

"I'm not here for you." Her voice hisses out, and I repeat the "snake hate" in my head. No way am I telling this nightmare come to life of my fears. She might be an enormous viper shifter for all I know.

Pinning me with a black gaze that has no white, she looks as if she must be blind except she's staring right at me. Yep, I'm gonna keep looking at her onyx eyes and not the blood tears coming from them. I know now where the metallic stench came from.

"Can I help you find whoever you're looking for?" I offer. *Then, perhaps you can get the hell out of my city and swamp.*

"No need, shifter." Her voice cracks and splinters, the hiss unraveling into a chorus of terrible singsong beauty. She cocks her head, those dark eyes yanking at me like a black hole's gravitational pull.

This freaky lady might be more horrifying than the seven Houses put together. My throat closes around a growl, but I manage a quick nod.

She draws her wings to the side, as though she's sweeping away heavy curtains with a mere flex of her shoulders. "I'm here for her."

Sprawled on the ground at her feet lays a crumpled heap of human. I yank my gaze from the bigger predator to risk a quick peek at whoever isn't getting up. A ponytail slick with blood spills in a gruesome halo.

*No.* I hurry forward, taking in the heart-shaped face and, under the stink of blood, the whiff of rose-perfumed shampoo. My world tips on its side, my vision narrowing to that ponytail and cold darkness. I go to my knees, the hard gravel digging through my jeans, but I can't care anymore. My heart seizes, missing a beat or two that might've been important a minute ago but won't matter now. Not when the girl it'd beat for all these years is gone.

"Dottie." I can't say her name without my voice shattering the same as everything else within me.

"You knew her?" Past tense. Whoever this creature is, she's sure that my girl isn't here anymore. Only her body remains.

"Yeah." I drag the word up through years of memories. Dottie smiling at me in sunlight, the golden glow catching on her hair. Us passing notes in class, coded so any intercepting teachers wouldn't report the bad shit going down at both our homes. Her lacing her delicate fingers in my bigger, rougher ones. Her trusting me without knowing what I was beneath the human façade, but still understanding me more than anyone else.

The raw pain of grief stabs at me again and again, a fight of invisible teeth and claws, one I can't win. "I knew her."

"You would find the one who killed her?"

"Hell yeah." I consider my phrasing, but if the scary lady came from hell, then maybe she can help me send whoever murdered Dottie straight to that eternal inferno on a one-way ticket. "I'll shred them into slivers." I raise my claws, keeping them tight against my body because whoever took off earlier, I can't hear them anymore. Taking a deep inhale, I can't smell anything over the blood.

"You were her champion?" The damn singsong in the creature's tone annoys me.

"Dottie didn't need a champion. I would've been if she'd let me." If I hadn't left her. "She took care of herself, her family, me." Or she had once. "Defended those who couldn't." Or wouldn't. No way had I wanted to draw more attention than absolutely necessary to myself in high school. Teenagers can spot *different* a thousand yards away, like snark-mouthed snipers.

The creature eyes Dottie's body with interest, and I can't stand the way she stares when my girl isn't here anymore to defend herself. "A fighter?" she asks.

"With a sharp tongue and long memory." I crowd the creature to get to Dottie, crouching beside my girl, not wanting her left out here in the dirt, although I shouldn't move her until the seven Houses are called in. The first death of a human—*my human*—in Syn City means the Syndicate will be involved in the aftermath. Unless...I stare at the creature. "Why do you ask if she's a fighter? Who are you?"

A snarl-tinged smile reveals long, sharp teeth. Yeah, so? I can break out fangs too. "I am someone who can bring her back. If she chooses, and if you'll help her find vengeance."

*Vengeance.*

By the gods, the blood and wings and penchant for black? This creature? She's one of the original three Furies, an immortal, a creator of the House of Furies here.

"I swear it," I say, rushing to accept. "I'll make any blood vow you need, just bring back my Dottie."

"If she accepts, she won't be yours anymore. She won't even be human." The Fury spreads her wings, shoving me away hard enough to knock anyone not born a cat shifter on their ass. "As a reborn daughter of mine, she'll be more."

"But she'd live." Right now, that's all I care about.

"She would, and she would serve as my other daughters do until she dies a second death. Not even I can save my children from that." Her finality spoken with such sadness hits me, but I shrug away the consequences of decades from now in exchange for Dottie breathing again.

"Please." I can count on my fingers the number of times I've said this word and truly meant it. "Whatever you want, I'll do. Whatever I have, you can take. Give her another chance. She didn't deserve this. No one deserves *this*." To have been attacked, murdered, and abandoned so ruthlessly. How could anyone be so cruel? I flinch. I'd been that cruel once, no matter how I could explain away what I'd done.

The Fury snaps her wings out, a screen to shield whatever she's doing. No way am I interfering with her death magic when I can barely breathe with equal parts hope and sorrow choking me. Seconds tick by like hours.

"It's done." The Fury vanishes. No goodbye. No aftercare instructions. No nothing. Just poof.

I scramble to Dottie's side. With her eyes closed and blood everywhere, I can't tell what the immortal did. "Fight," I whisper, gathering her into my arms. "I'll let you win every argument, eat the last candy in the box, tell me all my flaws in excruciating details. You can hate me forever if you'll only open your eyes. Don't make me blame myself any more than I always do. Come back and tell me off to my face for leaving you, for not protecting you, for everything."

Dottie's chest rises and falls, a movement so delicate and all-consuming that I can't look away, counting the thuds until she breathes again.

*Thank the gods.*

*Thank the Furies.*

The sound of wings flapping make me jerk my head up. What now? Oh no, Sadie "Slaya" Tucker and Kiva "Killa" Divine touch down beside me, spitting gravel that bites into my skin. Shielding Dottie, I manage to keep her face covered, but with blood slicked down the side of her head and trailing into her shirt, I can't tell if she has any new scrapes or cuts from those stinging, sharp rocks. *Shit.* I hadn't meant to call upon these Furies or any of their contemporaries with my silent prayers.

"This is unexpected." Sadie sounds bored and over it all, her high-class version of the all-black Fury uniform being designer high-heeled boots and a tailored suit that's probably bespoke. "But I'll take it." She stretches her hand, and an unfurled leather whip flies into her curled fingers, one so much like the whip that'd been curled at her creator's hip. Each Fury deity daughter has a magical weapon to call that comes in an instant and never misses. I'm not surprised that bossy, sadistic Sadie has a whip as hers.

"Hiya, kitty cat." Kiva gives me a *s'up* chin bob. Her version of the black uniform might as well be an icy longneck bottle of beer to Sadie's Bourbon Manhattan. Unlaced high-top sneakers so well worn that they're threadbare, ass-hugging jeans, and a T-shirt from a local country music star with the sleeves ripped off, the Fury could've come from the bar where I work rather than being a headlining favorite of the derby team.

"Been killing humans in our territory, shifter?" Sadie asks, icicles dripping from her tone. "I can't believe you were stupid enough to stick around for us to catch you."

"He's not," Kiva answers before I can get a word out. "Look past your shifter hate for a sec. He didn't do this. Dude's torn up about her death."

"Whatever." Sadie taps manicured nails against her whip. "I still say we haul him in for questioning."

Rolling her eyes to the sky as if seeking patience from the creature who just left in dealing with her sister, Kiva crouches next to me, pulling her wings in and disappearing them. Her face softens, her badass destroyer-on-the-rink frown dropping to something akin to concern. Or worse, pity. "Let us see her, Chase. We can't take revenge on her killer until we know who or what we're dealing with."

"Dottie's alive." I relax my hold the least little bit. No way am I letting her go until I know she's safe.

The incessant *tap-tap-tap* against a hard leather handle stops. "How long you going to hold on to denial?" Sadie asks. "Because I hate to tell you—"

I cut into whatever crap she's dishing out. "One of your creators, an original Fury, she showed right after I came on the scene. Dottie was already..." My throat tightens around the word, my chest doing the same, as if I by speaking that hideous truth, I might wish it into being again.

"You saw the transformation?" Kiva gapes at me. "Zeus's big brass bolts, you witnessed an original Fury at a murder scene and lived to tell the story?"

"Uh, yeah." Now, they're both staring at me, and I struggle not to yank my girl up and run as far as my shifter speed might get us before they catch up. Not freakin' far, seeing as Furies and the other Houses basically have superpowers. Never mind the wings, Furies can be quick on foot, especially when they're tracking a target for their vengeance. "Your creator, she talked to me."

"You want us to believe one of the Big Three stopped to chat with you?" Sadie's still standing a few feet away. Maybe she's afraid she'll become shifter if she gets too close. Not that we're contagious, a fact the humans have proved a hundred times over by trapping and studying my kind in their labs. "Why would an immortal talk to you?"

"She asked whether I would track the killer, whether Dottie was...is a fighter." Cuddling her closer against my chest, I find comfort in every breath my girl takes.

"Because you knew Dottie?" Kiva sounds so hauntingly wistful. "You know the life she had?" The question makes no sense to me until I realize I've never heard this Fury discuss her death or her first life.

Furies swap how-I-died stories like they're badges of honor because, in a way, they are. None of their house came into being without first suffering a brutal murder. It's the Fury way. For Killa Kiva, who has a big mouth and bigger presence, not to discuss her death, there must've been something unusually cruel about the method. Or she doesn't remember. I don't have time to ask about either possibility, not with her sister looking as though she wants to flay my skin off one crack of her whip at a time to see if there's fur hidden beneath.

"Dottie and I go way back," I say to Kiva. "We come from the same hometown."

"So she'll be happy to see you after she turns?"

My stomach sours. Such a simple question, but Kiva's not going to like the answer. Her sister will appreciate it even less. "Maybe." Half-assed answer, yeah, but better than the truth. "She was my best friend in high school." My only friend.

Coming closer to inspect the damage, Kiva whistles low. "That's a nasty skull wound. Let's hope that whack to her head didn't knock her memory out of her so she remembers your friendship."

I settle on telling the rest of the truth. "We, uh, didn't part on the best terms."

Sadie snickers a bitter, cruel sound. "Then we should let you hold on to her until she's through the turn."

Why would that be such a bad thing? I tighten my arms around Dottie, wanting to stay with her as long as possible, to see her wake up, to go down on my knees and apologize. "I won't leave her."

Kiva shakes her head. "We'll discuss why that's not happening in a second. First, I need to sort some stuff out. Maybe Coach got her prophecy wires mixed, but that's a rare thing. She thought we'd find a human *before* a murder happened. Instead, we run into you holding a recently dead girl. Want to tell us why you were out here and what you saw or heard or smelled with those shifter senses?"

"I thought I imagined her tonight at The Rink." I inhale, taking in the rose and sunshine and sweetness of Dottie beneath the blood. "My gut told me it was her even though I haven't seen her in years."

"Hades's hellfire," Sadie swears. "She's your mate."

"No." A human as my mate? My inner mountain lion wouldn't be dumb enough to go there, would he? Except I'd felt a pull to Dottie from the day we'd met that didn't leave me despite how much physical distance I put between us. "Maybe. I don't know."

Although I've focused on *not* thinking about Dottie since I last saw her, she's all I can think about. It wasn't this bad almost a decade ago. Though, if I'm being honest, I've thought about her every day since I left. Anyway, we'd have been too young to do anything if the "warning, shifter mate" alarm had gone nuclear back then. So maybe the Fates had been trying to protect me, or maybe the crazy destiny goddesses just wanted to wait and fuck with me now. She *can't* be my mate—not with the on-the-run life I live, with the exception of this temporary sanctuary in Syn City. Dottie deserves a better mate than me.

The Furies exchange a look that I can't read. There's an undercurrent to this conversation that I'm missing.

"What?" I demand, not caring if I piss off any of the Houses at this point. They failed to protect my girl, my human, despite their safety promises to keep guests coming to Syn City.

The two continue the stare off for another long, tense moment. Kiva breaks first. "The original Furies don't appear to anyone other than the chosen unless you're a fated or accepted mate. Either way, we're going to need to take her from you, at least for now."

"Why?" I squeeze Dottie as close as I can without risking putting another bruise on her. Her blood coats my shirt, sticky and smelling to high heavens, but I want her marking me because maybe then I can believe she's back with me. She's not my mate, but she matters to me. "I lost her, and I've only gotten her back. I'm not leaving her."

"The turn from human to Fury..." Kiva glances at Sadie's wings, rolls her shoulders where her own must weigh heavy although tucked away. "It isn't pretty."

"All the more reason for me to stay with her. What if she wakes up scared? Or confused?"

"She will," Sadie answers, the whip vanishing from her hand as easily as if she'd spelled the weapon away. "When she does, she'll need us. Not you."

Her rudeness has my cat's hackles rising as though bristling against my skin from inside. "I'm not afraid of a shift. Not of a shifter, not of a Fury."

"Oh, kitty cat," she drawls, a glossy polish that doesn't hide the hate. "You should be. Nothing's more than frightening than a fledgling Fury."

# 3

## DOTTIE

F EVERED HEAT CRAWLS OVER ME, SCORCHING MY SKIN AS THE BLAZE marches from my head to my heart and beyond. The inferno feels as if it'll burn me up from the inside out. I force my eyes open, blinking against the darkness. My heart thunders, adrenaline flooding my system no matter how many times I tell myself that flipping out won't solve anything.

Where am I? Why can't I see? And who dropped me in a volcano? The itching between my shoulder blades screams, a stinging worse than falling off my bike on a country gravel road where the rocks cracked open my knees and palms. The childhood memory races to connect other, more recent, violent ones in a chemical reaction that'll eat through anything in its path like mixing drain cleaner and water.

I ran from whatever had been stalking me on the path to the bus stop. The last thing I remember was spinning toward someone or something—no face comes through clearly—right before I got clocked in the head.

Reaching for my head and neck, I make sure everything's where it should be. Foolish, I know, but I don't care right now. Panic ratchets up my spine, tensing my muscles in preparation for another fight or flight. Because if I didn't escape whatever came for me, then where in the seven hells am I now?

"Dottie, can you hear me?" A woman's drawl comes from nearby, smooth and cultured, money South as opposed to my backwoods twang. "Stay calm. The blindness doesn't last long. It's temporary for us all during the turn."

"What?" My voice cracks, my throat as raw as if I'd screamed my way through a monster truck rally to find Momma on one of her benders. Oh my gods, I *am* blind. "Did you knock my eyeballs out?" I don't care if I sound crazy. Somebody needs to give me answers. For all I know, I've been kidnapped by human traffickers like those in Connie's true crime stories. "Who are you? Where am I?"

"Get Coach," the posh snob continues as if I haven't spoken.

The phrase makes no sense to me, but she must've been talking to someone else in the room, which only ramps up my fear. There's more than one person here, and I can't see, my skin's on fire, and my back stings as if I'd been skewered by a hot poker. "What is happening?" My question comes out much too loud for my ears. I flinch from the agonizing pain.

"Move, Sadie. You're scaring the shit out of her," another woman says. Her voice holds none of the polished snobbery of the other's. No, she sounds New Jersey crossed with California in a bizarre twist that's as comforting as it is confusing. "Let me guess, rookie, you're feeling like someone soaked you in gas, lit a match, and ran you over for good measure?"

A horrific visual but... "Yeah. Did they?"

She snorts in an almost laugh that carries a lot of snark but no mean. "Nah, but it sure seems that way the first few minutes. Your body's adjusting. Someone snuck up on you while you were on the path to the bus stop."

"Who?" Because I have the overwhelming need to beat them senseless with whatever they used to wallop me. I've never had a nasty temper, but right now, I'm willing to give anger a try.

"Whoa." The cultured beauty queen sounds as if she's backing up. *Good, she should.* Beneath the hurt and fear, I feel stronger than ever. "Calm her down for satyrs' sake," she says. "What if she calls her weapon and comes at us? I'm not ending up twice dead for anyone. We already have one giant strike on our record, so the last thing we need is everyone thinking we couldn't take care of one fledgling Fury."

"Take care of—" My anger stutters to a stop, her last words replaying in my head. "A what?" *Nooo.* Visions of a woman in a dark dress with tattoos winding around her body in twisting black vines asking me to make a choice have me jerking to a sit. My head swims, dizziness shooting nausea through me. Unable to stop the sick, I retch and hate myself for the weakness.

"Ugh, she had the popcorn." Miss Fancy Pants obviously didn't leave fast enough to miss my mess.

"Lesson one, rookie," the other woman says, "don't eat the popcorn. We think it might be laced with cocaine the way the humans suck it down."

Fighting back the next round of sick, I keep everything, including a possible drug cocktail, on my stomach. "Sorry about that." Why am I apologizing? I'm the one with the massive head injury. But I can't stop myself. "Baking soda and dish soap will clean that right up."

"Good to know. I'm Kiva. The mouthy sorority girl's Sadie. You caught last night's show at The Rink?"

"Yeah." The pieces click together for me. I might've flunked math a time or two, but I'm a puzzle whiz. "You both skated. You're Killa, and she's Slaya, although she's coming across more scaredy-cat-who-can't-handle-vomit right now."

"Hey," Sadie snaps. Yep, she sounds madder than a drenched hen flapping at the water hose. "Watch it—"

"Yep, good memory." Kiva keeps talking like the other woman hadn't said a word. "What do you remember after the show?"

This part's a struggle, a mental scramble I have to work to

piece into a straight line of things that might've happened one after another. "I stuck around to catch the late bus." I'm not about to admit to these two why I needed to ride the cheapest transportation out of the city, especially not when Sadie sounds as if she might've been born with an entire silver set shoved in her mouth. "Bumped into the props manager on the way out."

"Marty. Nice guy."

"He was." I struggle to remember what we talked about. "He offered to find someone to walk me to the bus stop." He'd said other stuff, but what?

The beauty queen butts in. "Sounds like you should've taken him up on that instead of hooking up with a shifter."

"Shut up, Sadie." Kiva doesn't sound pissed off, just tired. "Go fake being useful. Find out what's taking Coach so long to get here." Footsteps stomp away, and a door slams. "Sorry about that. What next?"

"What'd she mean about a shifter?" I didn't hook up with anyone. Persephone's panties, I've never hooked up with anyone, and now Momma is set on marrying me off to the new preacher in town so I'll be stuck in Petunia forever. Except supernaturals like Furies aren't allowed in our town. My gut rolls again, and the burn pricks at my skin, but it's not as bad as before. "What'd she mean by fledgling Fury?"

"Promise you won't projectile puke again?" Kiva makes the question seem only half serious.

I don't know which scalds my skin worse, the embarrassment at getting sick all over celebrities or whatever super-premature hot flashes I'm having. "I'll do my best to control my gag reflex. Should be easier without the beauty queen. Although I can't see, so maybe she's fugly as a Gorgon. I wouldn't know."

"You and I are gonna be friends, rookie."

Under different circumstances, I'd be begging this woman for an autograph to give to Connie, but right now, I'm more worried I won't be able to go home again. "Momma will be worried if I don't make it back by dawn," I lie. My mother probably won't notice that I skipped town until payday.

"We can send someone to let her know where you are."

"No," I squeak, scared I'll be sick again. "No, that's all right. Just tell me what's going on. I remember the path to the bus stop." Earlier, she'd seemed set on making me recount what had happened after I left the show. so I'll spit out everything I can piece together. Maybe then I can leave. "I heard noises from the bushes and gravel crunching behind me, and I took off running." Frowning, I try to figure out what I heard, but my head hurts and the thoughts muddle together in a fog.

"Smart thinking, not sticking around."

"Syn City's safe for humans, or so everyone keeps saying, although no real safe place exists."

"Raised around violence?"

"We're women." I want to sigh, but my chest's too tight. Everything seems so darn heavy right now. "When's the world ever been safe?" It's the truth that has me suffocating in my hazmat suit most nights when I'm called to clean up yet another mess. "Weren't we all brought up with the threat of danger?"

"I don't know," Kiva says. "You'd have to talk to Sadie about that."

"Beauty queen can't have had too hard of a life." I've known plenty of girls like her—rich, entitled, and convinced of their suffering when they haven't gone to bed hungry a single night of their mansion-sheltered lives.

"Everyone in the House of Furies comes into the crew with their own cargo ship of emotional baggage whether they remember it or not. But we're talking about you. You heard noises and ran. What else?"

"Whoever it was, they'd gotten close, so I turned, ready to hold my own." I wait for her judgment about taking on someone who'd obviously beaten me or not having enough sense to keep running, but she doesn't fuss at me.

"Interesting," she says instead, as though I chose the most natural response in the world. "Go on."

Figures a Fury would be more stand and fight than run away and hide. "I couldn't see the person's face, didn't see much of anything except the big hammer coming at my head."

"A hammer means business like my hatchet." The way Kiva compares the two weapons that I'd rather think of as normal garden shed tools makes me want to curl into an invisible ball.

"Okay." I leave off the *crazy lady* part.

"Your attacker? Male, female, or somewhere in between? Human, supernatural, or unknown?"

"I don't know. I was staring at the hammer, not the psycho wielding it." Arguing with her isn't my smartest idea, but I've had a lot of dumb ones tonight.

"Hear anything else?"

"No." But I'm not telling the whole truth because somehow my delusional about-to-die brain conjured up Chase's voice calling my name, reminding me of the one friend I'd had, the one who'd left me, the one who'd never come back. "No, thankfully I must've missed the part where the hammer whacked me."

"It's probably for the best you blocked that out. Remember anything before waking up here?"

My eyes itch, the blackness fading into blurry images that make no sense. "Where's here?"

"The House of Furies."

"Shut. Up." People have offered more money than I'd make in a hundred lifetimes for a behind the scenes tour of this place. The Muses might offer reality show glimpses of their gilded mansion, but no one has come through the Fury House. Or at least no one who lived to talk about the trip. "My cousin will flip out when I tell her."

"Yeah? She a fan? Stop touching your eyes. You'll make the itch worse."

"Connie's a superfan. What's going on with my body? How

much coke do they put in the popcorn?" Not that I'd know the difference between a speck and a pound. "I feel wrecked."

"Hate to break it to you. I figured you'd pick up on the clues, but apparently not." Kiva doesn't sound sorry. In fact, she sounds downright chipper. "You died."

"I what?" I mean, I'd had an idea in the most terrified, quietest, *shhh, pull up the covers and it'll go away* corner of my brain. But...what the actual fudge cakes? An even worse possibility—if there could be one—hits me. "Is this my hell?"

"While it may feel like it with all the drama in our House, no. The blow to your head killed you, but good news, one of the original Furies brought you back to life. Yay!"

I blink again, making out a hazy face with dark hair, silver glitter eyeshadow, and red lips. A maniacal cheerleader in goth getup has nothing on Kiva. "An original Fury? You mean the freaky lady with the snake tattoos."

"Shh." She claps a hand over my mouth, the smell of sour gummies strong in my nose.

"What?" My muffled question sounds more like *mwrr*.

"You can't say shit like that. The immortals who created us? Folks from ancient times didn't even call them Furies out of fear of them. You know they're the Underworld version of a soul-crushing death sentence for killers, rapists, and oath breakers, right? They chose you as a daughter, or at least one of them did, but they aren't the hippy peace-and-love kind of moms. They're more into the smite thee stuff, namely vengeance. *Capice?*"

I nod, having seen enough old gangster movies to understand the word.

"Cool." She pulls her hand away. "So welcome to the House of Furies. You know all seven Houses, right?"

"Uh." I choose my words carefully, not wanting to tempt the whole smite thing or have Kiva smothering me again. "Will there be a test? Connie would be way better at playing along if there is. Maybe I could message her?"

"Later. Just know our House is the best. Once you finish turning, we can get to work making you an awesome Fury."

"Turning? Like a vampire?" Or worse, a shifter.

"Nah, nothing like that. The rules are simple. You're part of a sisterhood now. Mess with one of us, you mess with all of us. We only go full-out vengeance when our blood calls to us because our goddesses have declared it's time to deliver payback. It's part of the Fury gig. Super cool, right?" She doesn't give me time to answer with an *oh my gods, I'll stab myself as klutzy as I am*. Nope, she keeps going. "We'll train you up, and you'll be a proper badass. The signs are already there with the way you reacted to your killer and how the original Fury chose you. Oh, and you'll skate."

"Wait a minute. Skate?" Of all the what-the-Hades horrors she'd ticked off like a grocery list, the last has me envisioning myself careening on four tiny wheels to slam into the steel rails surrounding the rink. Or worse, into a Huntress.

"Well, yeah, we all derby for the first five years after the turn as part of the House's contract with the Syndicate. You know, our governing council who rules us?"

No, I didn't know. Had this been mentioned in Connie's fan gossip sites? Maybe I should've paid closer attention to her celebrity babble. "Is there a class for this? Or maybe a guidebook?"

"Don't stress. Sadie and I will teach you everything you need to know."

That doesn't make me feel any better. If anything, the news that those two will be my spirit guides into this weird new world almost has me puking my popcorn again. "Uh, great." I don't sound convincing even to my own ringing ears. Despite the fact my back feels like it's been branded, I manage to roll to my stomach and push to a stand. "I appreciate the offer, but I'll just be on my way home. Thanks for everything."

"Whoa. You are home. *This* is your home. You can't go back to wherever you came from, not for years at least. It's part of the tradeoff for being brought back from the dead."

Pain at not being able to go home slices at me like a thousand tiny slashes across my scalding skin. My legs wobble, and I fall to my butt on the bed with an aching thud. Breath that should be coming in and out gets stuck somewhere between my lungs and my throat. Sure, I'd felt suffocated in my small town, but I hadn't thought about being exiled from it. What about my mom? She couldn't or wouldn't take care of herself. What about Connie? There has to be a workaround. I'll see how Kiva handled the separation and go from there. "You haven't been home since becoming a Fury?"

"Uh...." She looks away, and I wonder if I've somehow made things even more awkward with the only person I know here other than the beauty queen, and I can already tell that Sadie and I aren't destined to be besties.

"Sorry if I upset you. I just figured if you've made this—"

"I don't remember where my home is," Kiva says.

"What do you mean? Is it just me who..." What'd she call it? "Turned from human into this?" I can't accept yet that I may be one of those gorgeous women from The Rink. My reality doesn't line up with that fantasy. "Because I assumed the way you talked about people's prior baggage—"

"No, every Fury was human first, murdered, then brought back to life in Syn City no regardless of where she died. I'm the only one who doesn't remember her *before* life. Amnesia, the doctors say." She glances my way and takes in my shocked expression because, no, I couldn't wipe the OMG from my face. "Riiight? Who'd have thought amnesia could happen outside a soap opera like the one the Nymphs and Muses obsess over, *Covens to Covet*? The only reason I know my name was the bracelet they found on me."

"I'm so sorry." I'd been gearing up for a pity party over not being able to go back to Petunia where no one other than Connie has ever liked me much, and here's a woman with her entire history erased. "Is there anything they can do for you?"

She stares wide-eyed at me as though she's surprised I asked. "Uh, no. I mean I'm dealing okay, and I've got my Fury sisters, no matter how big of pains in the ass they might be. You can talk to your family soon, and they'll be able to come see you."

I've hit an all-time low if an amnesiac is comforting *me*. I work not to rub my eyes but give in to the need to scratch my stinging back. "Anything else I should know right now because I'm heading toward information overload? Gods, what's with my back? Did my killer stab me there?"

"Oh no, that's the best part." She glows like a kid on Christmas morning or Solstice or whatever the daughters of Greek myth legends celebrate. "Wait 'til you get your magical weapon to call and your wings pop out." She steps back, rolls her shoulders, and with a *whoosh,* out spring two massive black wings edged in deadly-looking silver blades.

I squeak, scrambling backward across the bed. "Those look lethal. Do they work? Can you fly?"

"Can I fly?" She says so deadpan and shoots me a sly grin. Smartass. With an *abracadabra* wave of her arms, she flaps her wings and—holy smokes—she floats a foot off the floor as though she'd stepped on a hoverboard.

"You *all* have wings?"

"*We* all have wings. You're one of us now. But no flying during derby unless it's a supernaturals-only, VIP event." She raises her fingers in air quotes with the last. "That's when we get to play the raptor shifters."

"Raptor shifters?" My voice cracks as visions of giants claws and massive beaks dance unwanted through my head.

"Oh yeah, we've got a big shifter population and tourist industry. Speaking of which…" She wiggles her eyebrows. "What's with you and the hot kitty cat?"

"Huh?" Maybe I could record myself asking *huh, what, uh* and press play for every future Fury conversation.

"The bartender?"

A prickle of unease races through me. "What?" See? Record, press play, repeat.

"Ya know, the cougar shifter, mountain lion, whatever you wanna call him—Chase Malone."

Knock me over with a Fury feather. I hadn't imagined him behind the bar at The Rink. Chase is *here*, and he's a freakin' cat shifter. "Wait, how'd you guess that Chase and I know each other?"

She twists a corner of her mouth into an evil Mad-Mae-worthy smile. "Seems I'm not the only one with secrets."

# 4

## CHASE

AT THE SWAMP'S SWELTERING EDGE, I RETRACE THE PATH FROM THE
Rink to the bus stop for the thousandth time this week. Battling
the monstrous mosquitos that grow freakishly large here, I circle
Dottie's murder scene looking for clues. Not that I find anything
that seems out of place. Not a single footprint, broken branch, or
crushed plant. Dust spits from the crunching gravel, and the
underbrush has soaked up any scents. Syn City's reputation as
the premier tourist destination with tons of foot traffic? Great for
business, shit for tracking a killer to fulfill my promise to an
immortal.

Aggravation sizzles in my gut as hot as a Southern summer
sun. Every day, I've gone to the House of Furies, and each time,
they tell me to go away. Actually, "go away" is a whole lot nicer
than what they say. If the Furies would let Dottie talk to me,
maybe she could give me clues, hope, or absolution.

Kiva and Sadie have appointed themselves as Dottie's
guardians, which makes no sense. Everyone knows those two are
the House of Furies fuckups, and they'd have been benched
permanently if they weren't the best players. Sadie hates me, but

she hates all shifters. Kiva seems to like me well enough, but she's not exactly easy to approach with her blade-sharp wings.

I wonder what Dottie's wings look like. Maybe fluffy and feathery? My mountain lion loves the idea of nuzzling close to such softness, then stalking her when she flies away.

*Nope.*

I need to shut down that line of thought. I can't fantasize about Dottie any more now than I have every single day for the last nine years. What if she doesn't want to see me? What if she's why I've been turned away from the House of Furies?

While that would hurt, it's better than my worries about what else could've happened. What if Dottie didn't do well in her turn from human to Fury? The ache in my chest overwhelms me, and I take to high ground, scaling a tree with my claws as if I can climb away the pain.

A rustle from nearby has me spinning, ready to fight.

"What's new, pussycat?" Kiva dangles her legs from the branch of a bald cypress tree as casually as if she's sitting in a regular chair.

"Damnit, I could've killed you." I curl my claws into my human skin, mad that I'd been jumpy enough to point them her way in the first place. "What are you doing?"

"Get it? Pussycat, mountain lion shifter." She frowns. "What? No smile? No laugh? Nothing?"

I glare.

"Fine, buzzkill." She heaves a weary sigh that says I've offended her in the worst way.

Whatever. I'll put the imaginary insult on my growing list of shit to deal with. "How's Dottie? Can I see her yet?"

"*I'm* fine, Romeo. Thanks for asking. I could use more work on my J-block on the track although Sadie's gonna have sore boobs for days with my last hit in this morning's training, but—"

"Dottie died less than a week ago. You didn't. So stay on topic or get the hell out of my way."

"What're you doing out here anyway? You haven't been at any of the practices to see my awesomeness. Other than stalking our house, you've been stomping around on this dirty path. Planning an escape or a night swim through the swamp and across the lake? Because sea hags seem the type to hold a grudge for all those kitties who've tormented goldfish for ages. They'd drag your pretty self to the bottom of the—"

I jump onto the branch next to her just to shut her up. My weight jars the tree, and she squawks, shooting out her wings to stay upright.

"Asshole!" She gives a hiss so surprisingly cat-like that I'm almost impressed.

I'm close to growling at the woman, Fury or not. "I'm searching for clues to track Dottie's killer since y'all don't seem capable of seeking actual justice even though it's your one real job. More than roller derby will ever be."

"Hush your mouth. Don't speak ill of my sport."

I snarl. "Leave if you can't help."

"Save the beastie crap for some girl who's down with that. I merely stopped by to tell you that Coach says you can see Dottie tonight after your shift, but if you're not interested..." She trails off, pretending to glance at her nails, but I don't need to be a cat to know she's playing with me, that she's aware she holds my full attention.

"Just tell me where to be."

"At the house where we can keep an eye on both of you since she's still vulnerable."

"I wouldn't hurt her."

"Yeah, I know, big guy, but some of the others don't believe that yet."

"You mean Sadie. What's she got against shifters anyway?"

Kiva shakes her head. "Her secret. She keeps mine. I don't rat hers. It's the Fury code, not a single snitch bitch in our house.

Unlike the friggin' Muses." Unfurling her wings with a snap that startles crows overhead, she floats away from the tree.

Yeah, yeah, she's cool. While I can climb and leap with the best of them, cats can't fly.

She flaps her silver-tipped feathers. "See ya tonight, lover boy."

My nerves hum throughout the dragging day and still buzz when I arrive at the House of Furies. Designed to intimidate, they haven't settled for the gilded mansion of the Muses or the lagoon-like home of the Nymphs. No, they've built a damn tree house that sprawls like some kind of eco-heaven built beneath the canopies of the leafy swamp cover.

Claws out, I climb the tree to the house for the seventh day in a row. Usually, this is the part where I'm kicked out by Sadie and company with a "get lost," "no boys allowed," or "she doesn't hang with the likes of you anymore." I tense, waiting for the same unwelcome committee at the front door that has more wards than a witch coven's lair. But no one comes.

Do I pound on the door? Announce my presence? Yell hello? I haven't needed to do anything before. In fact, I'd become paranoid that they have hidden cameras the way Sadie kept popping out the moment I hit the ledge on prior nights. At least they couldn't poof in and out like their immortal mom.

"You gonna stand there staring at our door?" Kiva's voice comes from above, and I crane my neck to look up—waaay up. She's sitting on the roof, swinging her legs like a demented demon child. "Don't be a scaredy cat."

Again, with the cougar jokes. "You writing a book of shifter humor for humans?"

"Nope." She drops beside me, her sneakers squeaking on the wooden platform. "Although I should. I'm hilarious. Let's go before Sadie escapes her chains."

I'm not asking because she sounds as though tying up a housemate is totally normal. Instead, I follow her, keeping my mouth shut when I have a billion questions about Dottie, about this place. The interior looks gigantic and luxurious, a sweeping stain-glassed ceiling above. Multiple staircases twist along each wall, leading in every direction like a labyrinth. Planks creak beneath my steps, and the smell of wood, cleaners, and nature soothe me. There's no A/C humming, but the inside is cool without being cold.

"You'll be meeting the rookie in our training hall." Kiva motions me toward one of the narrow staircases and bounces up the first few steps. I almost slam into her tucked wings when she stops. "Tell anyone what you see, and we'll have to kill you."

"Okay." I'm not sure how to take anything she says at this point. She could be deadly serious, or she could be yanking my tail. Either way, I nod, relieved when she moves again. "I didn't know you have a roller rink in the house."

"Not *that* kind of training, silly kitty." She steps up to a closed door, her face looking blue and purple in the cast of the stained glass overhead.

Having no idea what to expect, I steady myself. They could have a warded cell in there capable of caging my cat or a torture chamber given the Furies' love of torment. Friggin' hell, they could have a dragon locked inside. Not that I've ever seen one other than in holograms, but in the history of the Witching Wars, there's a dragon living in Los Angeles. I take a deep inhale and push down my suspicions. While my cat would rather be the one to do any stalking or ambushing, I need to go inside if I'm going to have a chance to talk to Dottie.

Kiva looks up at me. "This is where I leave you. Remember, you're sworn to secrecy by the same non-disclosure dealio that keeps your girl safe. Later." Opening the door, she jumps from the staircase railing to take flight in the massive foyer.

Bracing for anything, I step inside the dark room, my cat vision taking over to let me see in the low light. Punching bags and scarred mannequins crowd one area, weapon racks dominate another, and targets marked like giant dartboards line the far wall. Dottie hurls knives toward the bull's eye, missing badly unless she'd been aiming at the blank wall between the targets.

"Hey." I keep my voice soft, non-threatening. No need to startle the woman with blades in her hands. She takes a long breath, the sound wrapping around me, but I can't tell if it means she's focusing on the target, calming her mind, or preparing to skewer me. Still, I don't move. Even without the dim light, I would've known her anywhere. She smells like rose petals, like home. My cat wants to rub his needy self against her and purr, to make sure she's safe, to let her know how much I've missed her. But I lost that right years ago. "It's good to see you."

Oh so slowly, she turns to face me, pushing a button on her techie wrist gauntlet that brings up the lights. "It's been a long time, Chase." Her greeting might be nice, courteous, a distant hello to an almost stranger, but the steel tone beneath the pleasantry has my gut dropping, my lungs shriveling, and my cat wanting to flatten my ears against my skull if he could.

I can't pinpoint what she's broadcasting, whether it's disinterest, disappointment, or disgust, so I keep my distance. Pacing around the perimeter, I pretend that I'm taking in the room. But, in truth, my senses are soaking her in like sunshine after years of fog and rain. The easy quiet that came so naturally for us before hangs heavy and suffocating between us now. "How you holding up?" Dumb question, I know, but it's something other than the smothering silence.

"Kiva said you wanted to talk to me, which makes me wonder why after all this time." She rocks back on one foot, the floorboards creaking beneath her shifted weight. Gods, she's prettier than ever, all long legs and killer curves and soulful dark eyes. "She also said you've been here every day, that you were the first to find me when I was murdered."

"After." My throat closes around the word. *After you were murdered.* I work to push aside the memory of her bloodied and beaten on the ground. She's here now, alive with questions and maybe some answers if we're both lucky. "I haven't been able to track your killer so far, but I'll keep looking."

"Why would you?" She doesn't sound as if she's being mean or insensitive, just as curious as any cat. "What's in this for you?"

*You. You're everything for me.* I don't say the words aloud, not when she'd likely throw them back at me. "I promised your creator that I would hunt your killer down."

"You made a vow to a deity? Not smart. I'm finding it carries lots of responsibilities you couldn't have considered." Her voice drops to an almost whisper with the gravity of a confession.

The ten-ton, gods-awful reality smacks me over the head. I'd pledged a blood vow, but had she done the same? "Who'd you promise? What'd you promise?" And can I take whatever price for those oaths on myself so she won't be weighed down by them?

"Becoming a Fury meant I had to agree to be turned, to punish those that the immortal three deem need to be punished. Revenge and roller derby, the great Fury way." She shakes her head. "Guess I should've read the fine print before I agreed, only I didn't much want to be dead anymore."

"But you're alive."

She shoots me a look that says she doesn't appreciate my "glass half full" being better than a shattered glass outlook. "Silly me," she says. "I thought Syn City might have police, the same as we humans, although I guess I can't count myself as human anymore. Or maybe they'd have marshals like the shifters do— someone experienced with following rules for investigating crimes and taking down killers. But nope, in this town, apparently, the Furies are the law."

"The Syndicate relies on others for little stuff, but yeah, the Furies handle the big crimes here. Not that we've had any." I gesture toward the blade she's gripping like the weapon has done her wrong, better she be mad at it than me. "Want to tell me why you're hurling knives across the room?"

"I'm practicing for the less talked-about half of my new job, the one other than roller derby." She makes a *pff-shaw* noise that conveys more of her disgust for her new role than her words. "Tossing sharp stuff at a straw target is hard enough. How will I feel if they make me hurt someone? I don't know if I can do that."

"It's not your nature, never has been." It's mine. My shifter-born legacy of fangs and claws and blood doesn't translate to Dottie's world. She's sweetness, light, and all the things beautiful I've ever known. My cockiness is an act, a cover that I flash with lazy cat confidence. But *her* goodness? It's bone deep. "Can someone else do the job for you?"

She looks my way—seeming to see through to the heart of me like she always did. "You offering to be my champion like the knights in those old movies we used to watch?"

"Yeah, if you'll let me."

"The last time I trusted you, that I counted on you? You didn't show up." She raises her hand as if to keep me from interrupting, blessedly palming the knife so the pointy end isn't aimed at me. "Before you say anything, know that I stayed at that bus stop for hours waiting for you. Every hour of every day for the next year, I looked for you. I don't believe I ever stopped looking, to be honest. Thinking I saw you behind the bar when I walked into The Rink the other night, I figured I had to be ridiculous levels of stupid to keep seeing you almost a decade after you left."

"I sensed you there. It'd been nine long years, but I knew it had to be you."

"Oh yeah?"

When she steps closer, I talk faster, my nerves taking over. "I thought I'd lost my mind, but your scent's still the same."

"Well, that's creepy, though you being a shifter explains a lot."

My stomach bottoms out, and my heart knocks against my ribs, a trapped animal trying to break out of the cage to get to her. *She knows what I am.* "The Furies told you." It's not astrophysics. She's been here at the house since she turned, so unless she found out before coming to Syn City or during her tragically short walk after she left The Rink, it's the only logical guess.

"They did. I've learned a lot these last days. What I want to know is why you didn't tell me. We were friends for years, and shifters are born, not made, no matter what lies the haters might try to spin."

My cat claws inside my skin with the need to go to her, to comfort her, to convince her that I'm worth a second chance, but my human mind spins with all the possible excuses and reasons I can't tell her about my murderous predator nature. I settle on siding with my two-legged half. "I couldn't." From her narrowed eyes and the quick surge of spicy in her scent—anger or hate, it's hard to know which—I realize I should've sided with my cat and kept my dumb mouth shut other than *I'm sorry* or *let me earn back your sugary smiles.*

"Just like you couldn't come find me at The Rink even though your supernatural senses were screaming I was there?"

"I..." Too late, I put together that her questions so far have been a trap, one I skipped into with my unobservant human self. Panic has my cat pacing so viciously, snarling in my head about how he feels being stuck inside instead of shifting right here, right now.

She shakes her head, in an instant, her scent switching to sorrow. "Which would you like to explain first because it seems you've got excuses for the last nine years? Want to start with why you abandoned me in Petunia? I thought we were friends."

And I'd hoped we'd been more than that, but I would take whatever she'd be willing to give now. Except I have no idea how to convince her of anything.

She rolls her shoulders, and I half-expect wings to pop out, but nothing changes but for that get-out-of-here set of her jaw. "Gee, Chase, can't even answer that?" Crowding me, she pokes her daisy-painted nails into my chest. "What's the matter? Big bad kitty cat got your tongue?"

The last has me pulling her closer at shifter speed, grabbing those knives. I can't risk her accidentally cutting herself. The thought of her losing any more blood chills the hot rush of temptation. "Don't mess with my cat unless you're ready to play. He's not so nice, but he's patient."

Her scent changes again, not fear from my sudden supernatural speed. No, it's arousal. Huh, I hadn't expected that one. Maybe Dottie's grown claws of her own while we've been apart. As a teenager, she would've cried if I'd snapped at her. But now, she's sizing me up like a snack, one she might try for a few minutes and toss aside.

I back off. Yeah, I want a lot from her, more than a quick kiss or nibble, certainly more than she'd be willing to give me right now. "You've been hanging out with Kiva too much this week if you're borrowing her crappy jokes."

"You sound jealous of who I'm spending time with." She kicks up her chin as if challenging me when she's not so sure she should be. But I like the confidence. Cats don't value much, but we understand pride and vanity. I'm almost ready to ask her if we can start over, this time in a civilized conversation or maybe a well-placed grovel on my part. Instead, she rushes to speak before I can, saying, "If you wanted the right to be jealous, you should've done something about that in the last decade or so."

I can't with her. My cat won't let me walk away, and I'm not about to lie to her. I never did before—if we aren't counting the whole sworn-to-secrecy shifter thing, which I'm not. So I speak the truth no matter how much a murder may make her hate me. "What do you want me to tell you, Dot? How I came into the full powers of my shifter scariness that full moon? That me being the only child of an alpha threatened other idiot cougars—namely my stepfather—so he attacked me? How he ended up dead after slicing up my mom when she got between us?" My throat tightens, and my mouth goes dry. My body or my heart stops me from being able to admit to *this* woman that *I* killed my stepfather.

Her big brown eyes go sad, filling with pity that I don't want or deserve. "I'm sorry about your stepdad despite him being meaner than a snake and twice as lowdown. Your Ma...is she okay?" Dottie drawls out the last word in her twang that sounds like everything I want to remember about my teenage years. Her worry is a lifeline, and I grab hold.

"She's all right. You know Ma, she can bounce back from anything. If I'd given her another five seconds, she swears she'd have clawed that sumbitch's face off for touching her boy." I do my best impersonation of my mom. "As of our last weekly chat, she's doing fine."

"You talk to her every week?" There's a longing in her voice— not for me, no, but I'll take it. My Ma's tough, but she's not mean unless she needs to be, not like Dottie's mother, and I'm not mentioning her. I don't need to give my girl another reason to be mad at me.

"I know better than to miss our appointed chat time. During those years on the run, Ma was the only person I could count on even if she once threatened to claw my cheek if I decided that I was too important to talk to my mother on a regular basis."

"She did not. You're making that up."

"I swear she did, said I'm too pretty for my own good and could use a few scars. Gotta love Ma."

Dottie's lips twitch. It's not a smile, but she's not ready to stab me or toss me out of the Furies' tree house, so I count it as progress. "Can we start over?" I ask, testing the muddy, murky waters. "Maybe you can reassure me that you've been feeling okay since I held you all bloodied on the path last week. I'd appreciate it."

"I—"

The door *thwacks* open, and I reel, putting myself between Dottie and whoever might be coming in. A long, low laugh rolls through the room, and I fight the instinct to unsheathe my claws against the other alpha predator walking in.

With her hands on her hips and her silver hair pulled into a loose topknot, the woman stares at me through solid black eyes, no hint of white. The last I heard, she wields a giant battle ax as her magical weapon to call, and I'm glad she doesn't have it now with that Fury-blown gaze. "Well, well," she murmurs. "Look what the mountain cat dragged in."

# 5

## DOTTIE

COACH SHOWING UP IN THE DOORWAY HAS TO BE A SIGN. I MEAN what else could it be when she walks in right as Chase's about to convince me to start over with that easygoing, aw-shucks style I'd loved as a teenager? He's filled out since then with broad shoulders, a trim waist, and a body made for sin. The man's hotter than a mid-July noon with no fans and no shade.

From the way Coach eyes him like he might grab me and run, she isn't impressed with his movie-star good looks. I could tell her he's not interested in stealing me away, Fury or not. We've done this dance before, and despite what might've happened with his awful stepdad and amazing mom, he left me standing alone in the rain waiting for him to show up. No matter how he bats those lush lashes over gorgeous green eyes at me now, it doesn't sweep aside nine long years when he could've looked me up.

"Hiya, Coach," Chase says, stepping aside.

Huh, guess I don't need to introduce these two.

"Don't get any ideas about being the kitty with the canary, Chase. Our rookie's no pretty little bird singing all alone in a gilded cage. She's a Fury. Mess with her and the whole house will

take their vengeance out of your fur." Coach's gaze pins me to the
spot like a stabbed butterfly, but at least her eyes go back light
brown instead of black. "You done missing the target, Dottie?"
Her voice comes out soft, teasing.

"Yes, ma'am." Gah, everyone knows I'm not cut out to be a
weapon-wielding badass of justice. Nope, not me. I'm just the
klutz who somehow ended up in the scary house. Out of a
hundred throws, I didn't hit the center of the targets once. In fact,
I might've hit the wrong wall a time or two, but I'm not admitting
that to anyone. Not when Kiva can hit the center with her back
turned when she's tossing her hatchet, and Sadie can crack a
playing card in half with her whip. That last trick pissed off the
crew planning to play poker with those cards.

"I think we can rule out throwing knives as your weapon to
call." Coach eyes the room as if she can spot the scars in the walls
where I threw wide. "Why don't y'all both come to my office
where we can chat?" It's not a suggestion. No, she's already leaving, and that's an order to follow if I've ever heard one phrased so
sweetly.

I glance at Chase, wondering if he has any clue what this is
about, but he lifts a shoulder in a *whatever* movement that's so
very cat. Wondering how I missed the signs of him being a shifter
when we were teens, I follow Coach from the training hall,
wishing I had a fraction of her ease and self-esteem. "Is this why
you showed up tonight? To talk with Coach?" I ask him, working
to keep my voice low despite the noise of a party cranking to life
downstairs.

"No, I'm here for you." He leans closer. "Your housemates are
rowdy, but you don't have to whisper-yell."

"Huh?"

He touches his ear. Oh yeah, shifter sensitive hearing.

I swear he's so close that his hair sweeps against my temple,
and I can't decide if I want to snuggle with him or smack him. "If

you have super ears, then there's no need to cuddle." I try to make the last sound like a dirty word.

"But my cat wants to." His eyes flash gold behind the usual green.

Will I ever get used to this new version of my old friend? Of course, when he walks ahead to get the door for me, filling out his jeans in ways I shouldn't be noticing, I don't mind the improvements.

"Hurry up, you two." Coach sounds impatient. I've only been here a few days, but I know that's a bad sign, usually having little to do with me and everything to do with my roommates. The House of Furies fully embraces the original three-sister structure from the immortals. Coach divides us into triads, the new sisters we never wanted and probably wouldn't have picked. I'm stuck with Sadie and Kiva, who seem to stay in trouble.

As if my thoughts call them out of the house's twisting hallways, they both wait outside Coach's office. I don't ask if they're joining us because I'd rather not have an audience to whatever has rated as important enough to drag me and Chase in for a meeting. My heart speeds up, and my stomach twists the same as when I'd been called to the principal's office in school for whatever new crap my mother had stirred up.

Coach walks past my new sisters. They move to follow her, but she holds up a hand, as if she has the teacher talent of seeing troublemakers no matter that she's facing the other way. More than ever, dread bubbles in my gut, drumming up the memories of the *"Ooh, you're in trouble"* taunt of other kids in class whenever I'd get summoned to the school office. I'm ready to get this over with, whatever it is.

Letting me and Chase pass by her into the office, Coach calls out to Kiva and Sadie, "I'm sure y'all have found Dottie's killer if you have time to pester me. No? Then get to work." She raises her voice. "Party's over, Furies. Go find me someone who deserves our vengeance. Maizie, take the lead."

If I were to dream up a badass fantasy who could lead us into an apocalypse and back with a *we've got this* calm? It'd be Maizie, who fits the Furies poster girl description. With dread locks, brown skin, muscles that show she's a roller derby demon, and a flaming sword as her weapon to call that makes her look like an avenging angel in the stories, she's Coach's favorite. Too bad the WannaBe (But Never Will Be) Queen twins—Kiva's name for them—who make up the rest of her triad aren't nearly so cool. No, Maizie got stuck with the Furies' version of mean girls on steroids with goddess complexes.

"Y'all heard her," Maizie orders. "Let's fly."

The blaring bass cuts out, and the sounds of flapping wings and snarky shouts from outside replace the driving rock anthems. Coach shuts the door with a soft *snick* that booms too loud in the sudden hush. I flinch and check out the room, looking anywhere but at Chase.

A real painting, not a holo-screen, hangs above a solid oak desk. The painting shows three winged women wielding torches and whips. Each has hollow blackness where their eyes should be, the emptiness reflecting an entire rainbow of sorrow and anger and righteous indignation. *The Original Furies.* They must be. I recognize one from what seems like a dream before I made her a promise and woke to this new life.

I take a deep breath of the lemony clean scent and look away from the immortals, seeking something more comforting. An oversized couch takes up one wall with what looks to be a hand-stitched quilt draped over the back, and I wonder who sewed the piece of home for Coach. She has a collection of actual paper books, something I haven't seen outside of a school.

Photographs of all sizes cover every flat surface, and I think they might be family the way they're lovingly showcased in bunches. At first glance, the groupings don't seem to have any order with fancy golden holo-screens tossed in with popsicle-framed snapshots. The same faces repeat, but the bones structures, skin colors, and other physical traits don't. A large, adopted family, I realize. *Her Fury family.* I've never been part of a big family. Momma and Connie are my only kin from my life before, but now I have a house full of sisters and, by extension, their families.

Coach catches me looking over the flickering photos. "Nice to have somewhere to belong, isn't it, even if this isn't what you would've chosen for yourself?"

I nod, wondering if she can read my thoughts. The Furies all seem so fast, so strong, so perfect. Maybe some of them have more magic, especially the one who leads us all. "Did I do something wrong?" I ask her.

"Nope," she says. "I needed to talk to both of you without anyone listening at the door. They have a job, and they might as well do it while we chat." Glancing to Chase, she asks, "Any luck tracking Dottie's killer? I know you've been out on the path looking any hour that you haven't been beating on my door or working at the bar. Maybe you should try sleep." Pushing back in her chair as if settling in, she looks between the two of us. "Or maybe she's worth any sleep you've sacrificed since you've got some making up to her to do."

I want to interrupt, to tell her it's none of her business, but Chase answers, his deep voice wrapping me like a warm blanket.

"Dottie's worth everything; she always has been, but what's between us stays between us." Well dang, the man has big Zeus-worthy balls if he'll risk talking to Coach that way. "As for the killer," he says, "the scent's gone cold. I should've chased down whoever did this, but I couldn't leave her." He glances at me, pain and a request for forgiveness there in his deep green gaze. "Sorry, but seeing you there..." His voice trails off, but I don't interrupt, letting him sort through whatever emotions have stolen his words. "No way could I have left you. Not for anything."

The way he offers up the explanation as a confession, the

heartbreak in those words, I don't know how I'm going to hold on to the hurt I've carried for years.

"Let's get back to a killer being on the loose." Coach clearly isn't impressed by our touching little scene. "You know Syn City's reputation for being a human safe zone, offering a place for them to escape their realities while being guaranteed our protection. They come here wanting excitement and entertainment without any risk, and we give them a good time for a night, maybe two, if they stay in our pleasure district. Then, we send them home with empty pockets and good memories."

"Everyone knows that." Chase's tone screams get-to-the-point-already anxious, but I wouldn't have guessed any nerves with the lazy way he sprawls in his chair. I'm sitting at the edge of mine, my legs jiggling and my hands clenched. He looks like he's ready to switch on a holo-screen to watch a demon dodgeball game. "Syn City's reputation is why we all have jobs. Don't tell me an immortal turned Dottie into a Fury to keep the Houses' spotless record."

Oh my gods, I hadn't considered that possibility. My stomach churns, a sour sick coats my tongue, and I wish I hadn't polished off two bowls of jambalaya earlier. All the other Furies died somewhere else and woke up to their new life here. Had I been turned, not because I'd been chosen, but so I wouldn't become a statistic? All my life, I've been blamed for being born a girl, for not being nice enough, or for being too nice—whatever Momma's screw-up label of the day required. Is this simply a version 2.0 of the life I'd had? The life that some psycho stole from me?

"Did the immortals not pick me?" My voice comes out so much quieter than I intended, a tiptoe across the shattered shells of my ego. "Was I simply a problem that needed to be solved?"

"The immortals don't make mistakes when they're creating us," Coach says in a *"Don't be ridiculous,"* matter-of-fact way that doesn't leave room for argument. "Our mothers wanted you."

Chase reaches for me, his hand so close I can almost feel the warmth of him pulsing toward me. "She knew exactly what she was doing."

Another grim thought comes to me. "What if the immortals only changed me to make sure you promised to look for the killer? You're not some great hunter are you, or a part-time Sherlock masquerading as a bartender?" I rush ahead before he can say something like I'm being absurd or, worse, that he doesn't lie to me. Maybe not lie, but he has omitted huge parts of his life from the narrative of *us.* "I mean, you did keep the fact you were a shifter secret from me from the time you got to our school in the sixth grade until just a few days ago."

Chase's bored expression tightens to pissed-off predator. "I promised to find your killer *before* I knew who the immortal was and *before* she said she could bring you back. My wanting to slice apart anyone who hurt you had nothing to do with a bargain and everything to do with you—"

"All right." Coach's takes-no-crap vibe radiates off her, the cooler-than-you big sister who keeps everyone in line so we had better fall in or prepare to face consequences. "My comments about safety? Irrelevant to the immortals deciding to make you a Fury, missy." She sends an appraising look my way, then blasts Chase with an icy stare. "Are *you* the reason she jumps to self-critical conclusions like this?"

He shakes his head. "That's her mom's influence."

"Her mother that negative?" she asks him, completely leaving me out of the convo loop.

"She's all that and then some." He loses the angry vibe and goes back to looking like a between-films celebrity from the holo-pictures.

"Hmm, remind me not to put her on the invite list anytime soon," Coach says. "Back to my point before this turned into couple's counseling—"

Chase cuts her off. "We're not a couple."

His quick noping-out stings.

"You sure about that?" Coach asks. "Maybe you oughta reconsider seeing as how an immortal appeared to you, which is a privilege normally reserved for mates. Or is it that your cat's more worried about *her* rejecting you?" She holds up a hand. "I really don't care either way. All I need is for you to keep your kitty cat mouth shut if I'm sharing House secrets. Shifters won't say anything that would compromise their mate's safety, but if you're saying you can—."

He snarls something that sounds like a growled curse word. "I'm a mountain lion, not a house cat, and I'll keep Dottie's secrets to keep her safe."

"You did a bang-up job of that last time." Coach sounds like she might go full Fury on Chase and beat his ass into the ground if he wants to throw down.

I intervene because keeping the peace has been my lifelong job. "He said he wouldn't tell, and he knows better than to cross the House of Furies. Everyone does. You would send the Mad Maes to take his memories." Something I've learned in my short time here. The deity daughters of Dionysus, god of wine and madness, inherited much more dangerous gifts than a simple love of partying from their daddy. "And if they leave his mind broken, the Houses consider it collateral damage." Also a not-so-fun fact I discovered.

Their tense stare-off finally breaks with Coach picking up an electronic tablet from her desk. "Dottie isn't the first human to show up dead in Syn City these last few months, but she's the first to have been killed here. The Syndicate believes we have a serial killer in town."

Ugh, I might be sick again—no narc-laced popcorn needed. "Never mind my asking about being chosen." Moments ago, I'd wanted to be selected for a good reason, an *important* reason so badly. "Maybe I ought to be more careful what I wish for seeing as how a serial killer might've selected me for something sinister.

Who does that? Pick out random people to kill? And what makes you think the same person's doing multiple killings? Or that they murdered me?" I put my head in my hands, but I can't stop babbling. "Does anyone else think that makes me sound crazy since I'm sitting here alive and sort of well other than wanting to throw up from talking about this?"

The *kuh-shh* of a can popping has me looking up. Coach reaches across the desk, handing me a ginger ale. "You're not crazy. You're a Fury. Goodness knows, we're worse. We have excellent mental health care here covered by the Houses. As to being a deity's daughter? Well, you're stuck with the privilege until you die a second time. As for the serial killer, whoever it is has been leaving a body once a month."

"Full moon kills?" Chase asks.

Coach shakes her head. "The sixth day of every month, the regular human calendar and not the weird apocalyptic version some of the human cults adopted post Witching Wars. Trust me, we looked into all angles. Nor is this some rogue shifter or a teen who can't control their shift. There isn't enough damage. Although, if you go tracking a shifter, Chase, you'd be sucked into lion pride or shifter pack politics, no matter that you're a loner as a cougar."

"That's a definite risk," Chase says. "One I'd rather not take unless I absolutely have to. There have been a few unsolved shifter murders in recent years. Could be our killer has switched prey for some reason. How many deaths so far?"

"We've found four dead humans, and he makes sure to leave them where we'll see. We assume it's a male because of the strength needed to position the corpses." She meets my gaze. "Your murder happened on the sixth of this month, but I can't be sure that you were meant to be number five for the killer."

"Why not?" I ask.

"Because I interrupted him," Chase answers quietly. "The night I followed you, I sensed fear and ran toward you, not knowing for sure that I'd even seen you and hadn't dreamed you. When I heard your scream, I yelled for you."

My heart pounds, and I clutch at the icy cold and damp sweat of the soda can, needing to ground myself to the here and now. He had called my name. "I thought I imagined hearing your voice." As soon as the words are out, I want to snatch them back, knowing I revealed too much, but it's as though he's beyond worrying about what we might say or do to wreck each other all over again.

"No, that was me," he says. "I threw all my shifter speed into getting to you, but I couldn't go fast enough. You lay crumpled on the ground, blood everywhere, and..."

"Dead," I finish for him, so he won't have to say the word.

The silence stretches for what might be a few seconds but feels like forever with the house gone quiet and nothing but crickets chirping outside. A lightning bug zips by the narrow window above the couch.

I take a calming breath, then another when the first one doesn't help. "Other than the murders happening on the same date, what connects them?"

Coach taps the edge of her tablet. "I'll show you, but this information goes no further than the Fury house, you understand me?"

Almost regretting I asked, I nod and take the tablet. Four bodies with open but forever sightless eyes stare back at me from the screen, each dressed in distinctive roller derby gear and posed as if a grotesque art project. I want to look away, but I can't. The images blur in and out of focus, and it takes a few seconds before I realize it's me and not the screen. Had these women suffered? Had they been chased as I had? Had they felt the same terror as I did? In the rush of questions, an answer reveals itself to me. I jerk my gaze to Coach. "The killer's recreating Syn City's seven Houses."

She nods. "My guess is you'd have been the Fury, but he has

three to go, and we've got three weeks to stop him before the next kill."

Cold and hot rush over me, leaving clammy skin on my face and neck, a burning across my shoulder blades, and grim determination in my gut. I meet Chase's steady gaze and make my choice. "Where do we start?"

# 6

## CHASE

FROM THE MOMENT DOTTIE SAYS THE WORD *WE*, I'M ALL IN FOR finding this serial killer, no matter whether we're dealing with two different murderers or if the search drags me into shifter politics. Yeah, if I bring down the Furies on the wrong alpha's pet or if my stepfather's family finds me, I could wind up dead for my troubles. But when Dottie turned those big brown eyes my way and said *we*, my choice was made.

"I'm in," I say out loud, sealing my fate.

"All right." Coach sounds like she'd expected my agreement, which makes me wonder if she handed the tablet to Dottie because she's a Fury or because she could make me say yes to damn near anything.

Guess I'll never know. Coach wraps the meeting. "Until we figure out who killed you," she says to Dottie, "you're confined to the House of Furies or The Rink. When you leave this house, you're to have one of your roommates with you at all times."

Dottie scrunches her nose. "Sadie and Kiva already follow me everywhere."

"They'd better since those are my instructions." Coach gestures toward the door. "I'm not changing my mind, rookie. You can't be cleared yet for Fury missions, and I hear you've turned roller derby training into a literal crash course, so you'd better get to work. Chase, she has enough to do without you distracting her. Don't let me catch you tomcatting around my rookie." She kicks me out of the house a few minutes later.

Over the next week, I ask questions and listen to the rumors floating around the bars where I work at The Rink and in the pleasure district. Without being able to mention the dead or Dottie's murder, I'm stuck gathering intel on the sly.

Usually, I can score valuable information simply by watching and listening—who's cheating on whom, which of the Houses are fighting with each other, which deity daughters plan to double cross each other, the good dirt that folks only dish when liquor loosens tongues. I hear about some shifter murders out of state, but nothing about any serial killer or crimes in Syn City other than the usual suspects out to cheat the humans of their money. No mentions of ritual displays against the Houses, no rivalries outside the norm, no strangers hanging out in town other than the tourists who come and go on the daily.

I sweet-talk a bobcat shifter who works at the docks into letting me go over surveillance footage from the days surrounding the murders. Using the excuse of looking for an old friend who I'd thought I'd seen at The Rink, I scan through hours of the video but find nothing suspicious. With no new leads, I'm back to square one or maybe square zero.

Defeated, I swipe at the sweat from the sweltering heat and head toward The Rink to catch the first full Furies' practice session since the night of Dottie's murder. Locals and fans show up to cheer on their favorite House, maybe score a selfie and an autograph. I tell myself it's an opportunity to listen for gossip. But really, I'm hoping to see Dottie. She's been grounded at the House of Furies since the meeting with Coach, and I've been denied an invitation back, so I'll take my chances.

Stepping inside the building, the AC blows across my skin

like a cool cloth amid a fever dream, and the smell of cleaning solution overpowers everything else. While the janitors can open the place up to air mid-winter, there's nothing they can do in this oppressive heat to cover the sweat and body odor except mop, spray, scrub, and pray.

No one's on the track, so I sprawl across two plastic chairs only a few rows up from the rink that, come game nights, humans will shell out hundreds of dollars for the privilege of cramming their asses between the tiny armrests. I'm thinking of flipping up one more metal divider to really settle in when someone drops into the seat next to me. I don't have to look. My shifter senses go all tingly.

*Dottie.*

Ah crap, maybe the Furies have been on to something with the mates idea. The gods couldn't be so cruel as to coerce her Fury turn *and* stick her with a mate who still has a murderous debt due. Regret, want, guilt, and need collide in a brutal Molotov cocktail set to detonate in my chest. But she smells so good, her put-out sigh sounds like friggin' music, and gods, when I look her way, she's wearing black short-shorts and a cut-off shirt so tiny that it would fit a toddler. A winged pink skull and cross bones design sparkles across her breasts.

Dropping her skates into a chair, she props her booted feet on the back of the next row. Bruises and scrapes cover her arms and legs. Had she been attacked again? Why hadn't anyone told me? "Damn, Dottie what happened?" I work to not sound like an overprotective alphahole and fail.

"Roller derby happened. Everything hurts." She moves as if the mere act of breathing might be killing her. "Me sitting here doesn't mean we're friends again. I just can't go any farther down the darn stairs."

"You haven't rolled in a game yet, just practices. Why don't you use your wings to catch yourself?"

She shoots a you're-not-helpful crossed with a you're-not-the-boss-of-me glare my way. "Because I can't," she grumbles so low I almost miss what she says. Her side-eye screams all kinds of profanities she won't actually say.

"Why can't you? Since when are Furies sticklers about rules? Ever?"

"Since I'm the world's worst Fury. My wings haven't popped, not once. Maybe they're broken or jammed or something. I swear Sadie's ready to throw me out of a tree to see if I fly or fall to my second death. They've scared me, dumped cold water over me, thrown hatchets at me—"

"Hatchets?"

"Well, one hatchet. Kiva's weapon to call. Though I'm pretty sure she aimed wide. I'm fast, but not that fast."

"She used a magical, gods-granted weapon on you?"

Dottie shrugs as though tossing blades at each other's a norm in the House of Furies. Maybe it is. "Like I said, she didn't aim for me, or she'd have hit me. Furies don't miss with their weapons to call."

"Have you found your weapon yet? Maybe serve up some painful payback on her?"

"No weapons have chosen me. We've trained on everything from slingshots to spears to bow and arrow. Nothing clicks. I asked about a gun and got a lecture on how we aren't allowed to use those—something about the immortal code, but I suck at every antique weapon I try. Coach says it's all right, but she gives me this pitying looks when she thinks I can't see. No one else took this long for their wings or their weapon." She sounds so defeated that I want to make her smile, make her laugh, make her forget about those things.

"Something *has* to be going right."

"I can't become a full-fledged Fury without my wings and weapon which means I'm sort of stuck in limbo. I suck at derby, whoever murdered me is still out there, and I swear my room-mates have tried to kill me by teaching me how to skate in a tunnel they found. You know I thought maybe the Houses used hover skates. Nope, they skate with old-fashioned wheels on face-smashing concrete." She points to a shiner on her cheekbone, and I wince before I can stop myself.

"How's the healing? Did you receive any special abilities to help speed that along?"

"Oh yeah. We heal almost as fast as you." She ducks, looking around like someone might jump out of the empty section and scream *shifter*.

"It's cool. Everyone in Syn City knows what I am."

"You're a *who*, not a *what*. Don't talk like that about yourself."

Gods, I love when she gets all huffy, especially when she's defending me. "If you heal fast, what's with all the bruises?" *Abort, abort,* my brain shouts too late.

She gives me a look that says maybe she'll try out her weapons training on me. "I got these yesterday and today. The ones from the days before have already healed, just in time to make more right now at practice and my lap time trials. My healing's actually faster than most. I managed to clear the blindness during the turn in less than a day. Did you know our eyes go completely black when we're either talking to the original immortals or bringing down promised vengeance?"

Remembering the immortal who turned her, my throat goes tight and dry. "I hear it's part of the ready-to-smite package, a sign the original Furies give their deadly daughters that it's time to serve up an epic spanking."

"Well, then you should know better than to make me mad." Poking her finger at me, she screws up her face into an angry kitten one so adorable that I want to kiss her. My cat definitely agrees with that idea.

"Dottie?" A male voice calls to her as though he's seen the best surprise in his life, and my cat almost snarls.

"Hi Marty. It's good to see you again, without running over

you this time." She sounds so nice to him, almost as sweet as she once was with me. I hate him.

"What are you doing here?" Marty eyes me as though I've kidnapped her and forced her to The Rink. Or as if I might infect her with my shifter self. Not that I can, but some still believe the old myth. "I'd hoped to see you at another show, arrange some upgraded tickets for you down in these sections." *Without the riffraff*, says his glance my way.

"Oh, not-so-funny thing." She nods toward her skates. "I'm *in* the future shows."

He stares at her all-black outfit, his gaze lingering too long on the short hems. "You're a Fury?" His voice holds shock, awe, and *way-outta-my-league* realization, except he's still standing here gawking at my girl.

"Yeah." Dottie lets him down so sweetly, *too* sweetly. How does she know the props guy anyway?

"Hey, Marty," a Fury calls out, stomping down the stairs until she spots me. She's half of the idiot pair who hang around Maizie. Both of the twins zero in on me like a target acquired.

"Hiya, Chase," the first coos.

"How you doing?" the second adds as if they share one brain.

They pour sex and promises of pleasure into those sickly saccharine tones. "Fine, thanks." I fight a shudder and need a shower.

"Marty," the first snaps. "I need new knee pads that fit, not the cheap kind this time."

"That goes for both of us," the second says. "*Now.*"

"Uh..." Marty whips his gaze back to Dottie as if his head's mounted on a swivel. "Catch you later?" he asks her.

*No*, I want to answer.

But she smiles and waves as he leaves like the nice girl she is. Why can't she be awful every once in a while? To someone other than me?

"How do you know Marty?" I ask her, trying and failing to keep jealousy out of my voice.

"Met him the night of...you know." She doesn't need to say *her death*. "Sweet guy, but I think I shocked him by turning up Fury since I was human when we met."

"So Chase," the more nasal of the loser twins whines at me. "Want to keep us company later—"

With a *bang*, Kiva jumps from a row above to block the twins. "Going to stop you there, WannaBe One and WannaBe Two. Chase and the rookie are mated so move along before I tell Maizie that you two are hitting on a kitty cat instead of practicing the new block she taught you after you got your asses handed to you by the Huntresses in the last bout."

With a scowl and muttered "whatever"s, the two stomp down the stairs with as much noise as flip flops can make.

Dottie glares at her roommate as though wishing for her hatchet. "How many times do I have to tell you *we*—" She breaks off to wiggle her pointer finger between the two of us. "We aren't mated. There's been no mating happening here." Her voice is loud enough to make several heads turn in our direction, interests obviously piqued by the sex talk. Nothing attracts more attention in Syn City than who's banging who. "Um, I didn't, I mean, when I..." A blush steals up her neck to her cheeks, turning her skin a gorgeous "uh oh" glow. She looks to me for help.

Nope, she made this mess, she can turn the color of Persephone's pomegranates for all I care.

Kiva laughs and grabs Dottie by the arm. "Come on, rookie, before you give the WannaBe twins even more reason to hate you."

Dottie glances over her shoulder at me on her way down to the rink, and she makes the face she would right before she stuck out her tongue at me when we were kids, but we aren't kids anymore. A fact that's painfully obvious given the way she fills out those booty shorts. Nor are we friends anymore, which makes me sad, a lost connection severed years ago, yet I'd held on to a thin thread of hope that'll snap if she won't give me another chance.

I'll have to convince her I'm worth a gamble, that I won't take off on her this time. After all, an immortal trusted me to stick around, to find a murderer. Cold races up my spine and across my skin, making me swallow a snarl and leash the lion within who is clawing to find who bludgeoned his mate with a hammer. I don't argue with him about whether or not Dottie is our mate because I'm drowning in dread, and there's no time to waste on denial.

What if her killer comes back to finish what he started? What if he plans to deal my Dottie a second, *permanent* death?

# 7

# DOTTIE

CHASE SCOWLS AT ME FROM THE STANDS LIKE I'VE STOLEN HIS LAST snickerdoodle cookie. Yeah, I know, my ability to block the dirty blows of the WannaBe twins on the flat track leaves a lot to be desired, but no one wants their teen crush watching them suck so horribly at something. I'm not bad at roller derby; I'm a disaster.

"Rookie," Coach shouts...again. She's called me out at least five times in the last few laps. "How many times do I need to repeat the basic rules of the sport? The track's an oval, not a friggin' rectangle, and you're not the pivot, just a plain ole blocker. Your biggest job right now is to keep the opposing team's jammer—the skater with the star on her helmet—from passing you up and scoring a point. So maybe try blocking this time? I'm not even asking you to run a specific play or formation. Maizie, show her how a general block's done."

I watch Maizie move down the track with a graceful lethalness, a fluidity to her skating that allows her to go forward and backward with the same speed and ferocity. Her swift, powerful blocks are delivered like combat blows, but never to the illegal areas that seem to be all I can hit. A smack to the head, lower legs, or back of an opponent means a penalty, and based on my current playing, I'll spend more time careening into the side rails or sitting in the penalty box than actually playing. No way can I compete with Maizie-level skills or true deity daughters who can control their immortal-granted superpowers.

Unless super klutz becomes the Fury way, I'm out of luck.

"You've got this," Maizie calls, skating to a perfect toe-stop inches from me. "Stick to your drills, study the plays, and the rest will come."

*Sure.* But I don't want to disappoint her or give the WannaBe twins more reasons to make fun of me. So I try and fail again and again. I fall on my butt, knocking the air out of my lungs, only to scramble to my feet and go twenty more rounds.

"Take a break," Coach yells. "Rookie, over here." She points to a bench, and I fall more than sit. My hard *thump* echoes over the suddenly silent track. *Great.*

"Sorry," I mumble, but she waves away the apology.

"Let me see your wheels."

Staring at her, I wonder if she wants me to unlace and quit for the day, but she snaps her fingers and gestures for me to lift my leg into her waiting hand. "Okay." I stretch until I plunk my foot in her palm, thankful for once that I didn't outgrow my awkward long arms and legs phase. I wait for her to smack me like my mom does, but instead, she stares at the wheels attached to my low-tops as if they're talking to her.

"Marty," she hollers, and the prop manager comes running to her side.

"Yes, Coach?" he asks like an eager puppy, looking at her thankfully instead of my splayed stance.

Awesome, let's make sure everyone sees my colossal inability to do anything right. A glance up at the stands proves Chase's still there watching my every move.

Coach taps one of my wheels. "Bring her something less grippy, more slippy. These look as though they've been chewed up on ancient asphalt or a sewage grate." I don't share that both describe exactly how I've been training with Kiva and Sadie in the tunnels because that would mean admitting to Coach that I haven't stayed grounded like I was supposed to. Instead, I keep my mouth shut and listen as she continues inspecting my skates. "Go more narrow, but scuff 'em first, or she'll be sliding across the track and plowing into the pit crowd. Got it?"

"Yes, Coach." Marty sounds like a skipping repeat on a dance beat, but he takes off through one of the trap doors in the floor.

Looking up at Chase, I'm not surprised to find him meeting my gaze. He uses the same hands signs we did as kids to ask if I'm all right, to reassure me everything will be okay, and to see if I need him to come down. How can we act like a decade hadn't passed us by?

I've been carrying around tons of hurt and more than a little mad since he didn't show all those years ago, but what if he'd meant it when he said he couldn't? What if staying away for so long has been his way of trying to protect me? The more answers I get about him by asking around the House of Furies, the more questions I have. The concern in his cat-green eyes turns to plain just jealous green, and I want to demand, *"What gives with that?"*. I notice Marty heading my direction and check the impulse. No need to scare the props manager with whatever old drama Chase and I might rehash.

"Sorry if you caught me off guard earlier." Marty sits next to me, a different pair of black speed skates in his hands. "I didn't mean any offense. It's only that I didn't expect to see you again so soon."

*Or as a Fury,* I want to add but don't. He's been nice to me, and he knows this weird world that I've been tossed into much better than I do. So he could be a great friend with insider info who isn't a winged avenger looking for roller derby glory or someone burdened by the past that Chase and I share. "It's okay, Marty. As you can see, I'm not exactly prepared for all this."

"Yeah, I caught a couple of your wipeouts earlier." He turns his head but not before I catch his wince. "These should help." Flipping the skates, he takes out a scrap of sandpaper, roughing the smooth wheels. "The low-top leather version's the same style and size as you've got now, but Coach knows best on wheel selection."

"Are the wheels magical? Because that's the only way those might help me."

He chuckles an honest, strong knee-slap laugh at my joke, not *at me*, and his reaction relaxes me. No, his chuckle doesn't send shivers over me the way Chase's would, but it's a step toward friendship, and I could use all the friends I can get in a city where I'm the only recently-human, almost-Fury. "Thanks for this," I tell him.

"Of course." He doesn't glance up from his work. "Bringing out skates and props? Kind of my job."

"But being nice probably isn't in the job description, and I appreciate that you are anyway."

He stops and meets my gaze. "Not everyone in Syn City's as scary as your crew or the shifters, I promise. You'll get the hang of roller derby, and the rest will just come *super*-naturally."

"Good one." I tell him, switching out my skates for the new ones. The low top has a sweet padded curve under my ankle to keep the stiff leather from rubbing blisters, and its lighter than the other while still locking my foot in place. I can wiggle my toes without my ankle riding up. "Holy smokes, Marty, these are amazing."

"Top-of-the-line skates with both slip and grip. Easy enough to find in our stock in Fury black on black. The problems come when the Nymphs demand holographic neon and the Muses refuse to wear anything but pastels or candy colors. I can special order them, but you might've noticed how the Houses want everything done right now. Or yesterday."

"Yeah. Tell me about it. I've been here for two weeks now, and you'd think I've already screwed up enough for a decade."

"It'll all work out. You'll see. What's with you and the bartender?"

I follow his gaze to where Chase watches us as if we have a spotlight glaring over us. "Oh, I used to know him."

"You sure it's all past tense?" he asks.

*No.* Not given the way my heart speeds up whenever he's around or how he still feels like home. I can't even stay mad at the man. "Maybe," I hedge because I can't outright lie. "But I need to focus on my Fury future right now." I push to stand, shaky with the difference in the slide and slickness of the new skates.

Marty reaches out a hand to steady me, but at his touch, my stomach tightens, not in a good way, more in an oh-gods-I-might-fall-on-my-face clench that has me sucking in a steadying breath. I smile but the edges wobble, my lips curling downward. His casual touch the night we met didn't affect me this way, but I haven't been around a human since I was turned to Fury.

What if I can't have skin-to-skin contact with them the same way now that I'm a reincarnated retaliation and revenge war machine?

What if I can never hug my cousin Connie again?

A buzzing booms in my ears louder than hornets, sweat from my bad skating turns sticky cold, and worst-case scenarios whirl in my head faster than the super-charged washing machine we used after crime cleanups. I can't count the list of catastrophic crap that could happen now I'm on my second life.

"You okay?" Marty asks.

"Yep. Thanks." I sound like the squeaky squirrel in Connie's favorite video game, and tears burn my eyes. Rushing away so he won't ask again, I skate as fast as I can, as though I could outrun my own negative thoughts. Faster and faster, until the stands blur, until I zoom past Maizie and the others drilling, faster still, until I loop the track twice.

"Go, Dottie," Coach yells, and I throw on another burst of speed. "Don't stop. Give me one more. Move."

Letting fear fuel me, I race the irrational away until I know nothing but my pounding heart, hard breathing, and burning muscles.

"Yes!" Chase's cheer from the stands has me jerking my head up to catch a glimpse of the beaming smile I hear in his voice. The distraction costs me, and I shoot into the guardrail rimming the narrow crash zone, wrapping myself around the steel. Pain knocks my scream short and the air from my lungs. The jolt sends my skates flying out from under me and I go down hard against the slick polished concrete.

Stars explode in my flickering vision that switches from dark to colors to dark again like an out-of-whack hologram. My head rattles in my helmet, the chin strap digging into my skin in a blissful burn because at least my skull didn't crack in a second death.

"Breathe in slow through your nose, as deep as you can." Sadie's slow drawl comes from somewhere nearby. "Out through your mouth."

I turn to look, but the movement sends a sharp hurt rocketing through me, and a choppy gasp tears up and out of my throat.

"Uh uh, stay still, speed demon." Her voice soothes and calms in a way I wouldn't have expected from the beauty queen who earns her Slaya nickname on the rink. "Don't rush, and don't talk. Slow inhale, even exhale."

Hard thumps fill my ears. I swear the whole Nurse Sadie vibe slows my speeding heart, but no, those pounding thuds get louder and faster.

"Baby, you okay?" Chase's voice comes from right next to me. How'd he run so fast? Oh yeah, shifter speed. The *whomp, whomp, whomp* stops, and I realize my heart ticks fine. The thudding had been his booted footsteps sprinting out of the stands and across the track. The man must've vaulted over part of the rows and into the pit. "Talk to me, tell me you're all right."

"Keep your mouth shut, cat," Coach says, her voice so loud

that the mean in her tone makes me flinch. "You're the one who distracted her. You want to kill your mate?"

"I'm sorry, Dot." He sounds as if he regrets his entire existence, not just the last few seconds.

"S'okay," I whisper. Or at least I try, but the groan that comes out has me coughing and sputtering into a moan. At this rate, I'll be a walking collection of bruises, busted knees, and broken bones before my first bout of the season. Embarrassment makes the burn of pain worse. "Help me up."

"Let Sadie check you first." This time it's Kiva's voice. "She was a witch before she got offed."

Huh, I thought all Furies came from murdered humans. Wanting to ask the question, I open my mouth, but only manage to squawk, "Not human?"

Sadie shushes me. "As human as you were, but I practiced as a kitchen witch from a long line of healers."

"Like in the Witching Wars?" I can't check my *OMG* level of awe.

"Hardly." She makes an unladylike *pfft*. "Those pretenders out in LA who called themselves 'witches?' They're mages born to magical powers. Not a single one of them had to dig for intuition or learn spells and herbs and crystals from infancy." She stops ranting long enough to test my joints to make sure they still work. Thankfully, they do, although each movement throbs. "The women who burned during the wars, though? A lot of them were human-born healers just trying to help other people." Sadie sounds sad, and as of that moment, I don't want to know how she died.

"You're good, right?" Kiva asks me. "Nothing broken, and you're not dead again? Woohoo. Now tell your hot honey to get out of our space so we can get you vertical."

"The hell you will. I'll carry her." Chase practically growls, a deep rumble coming from him that he might mean to scare people, but I find the whole grumbly grump thing cute.

Sadie doesn't see the same adorable, not with the glare she gives him. "Read the room, cat. She needs to stand on her own, or with us."

I glance around, wincing with the ache but not wanting to scream, so yay for improvements. In the pit, the Furies have gone down on one knee. Only our triad remains on the rink, and Coach, who stands nearby. Even the few Gorgons here have taken a knee. "What're they doing?" I whisper.

"Respecting a downed derby sister," Kiva says. "If one of us is down, we all go down until she's up again."

"I can skate it off." I can. I will.

Sadie glances at Coach, then shakes her head. "I keep wolf's bane salve in my locker. Made it myself from an old family recipe. We'll patch you up with salve and ice until the doc can see you. Ready?"

"Yep." I'm not, but no way will I admit weakness in front of this crew. Glaring at Chase to keep him from sweeping in, I take the offered hands of my roommates, my triad sisters. They pull me to a rocky stand. Cheers and clapping echo around The Rink.

"Well done," Coach says. "The doc will need to clear you before you skate again, but I think we found your calling. You're fast." She purses her lips. "Dot—no, wait. Doll works with your cutie-pie looks and sweetheart charm. Doll Deadly. Furies, think we've found a name to replace rookie?"

Creative cursing might be an artform with Furies, and the *heck yeah* devolves into bad enough language to make me laugh despite the need to cry. Vertigo kicks in, and I lean hard into Kiva. Only I don't get far in my sway. No, Chase pulls me into his arms and sweeps me up against his chest. We're serenaded by catcalls aimed at him by the Furies with full pun intended as well as mocking wolf whistles because *haha* lions and wolves fight like cats and dogs. My newfound family doesn't skimp on the sarcasm.

"You made your point." His rough voice doesn't sound angry,

just worried kitty ready to prowl around the track unless he gets his way. "Let me hold you until my heart stops trying to fly out of my chest."

"All right." I pat him on the shoulder. "If it makes you happy." Because I hurt all over.

He darn near purrs beneath my touch, and I want to pet him again just to make him keep up that sweet noise. "Watch it. I might not ever let you go."

"Promises, promises." I shouldn't taunt a cat, but it's too much fun and I'm too dazed to care about the consequences.

"I'll remember you said that." He cuddles me closer, so close I can't tell where the burn of my red-faced mortification ends and his shifter super-heater begins.

The *suck-it-up-buttercup* perseverance that I've used to power me though the roughest cleaning jobs in my glamorous janitor job? Yeah, it's not working against the hurt hustle of my newfound life. While the crime scene cleanups and detox details of paranoid humans convinced they could "catch" supernatural germs might've been dirty, long hours of soreness and fatigue, I hadn't slammed into steel or faced rink rash from dragging my skin against concrete. Being inducted into this badass hall of fame is *hard*. But for the few minutes that it takes us to walk from the rink to the locker rooms, I breathe in Chase's familiar woods-after-rain scent, and the comforting connection of our childhood eases a bit of the pounding pain that's keeping time with my heartbeat.

Here, I'm safe.

Here, I'm home.

Here, I know Chase wouldn't let anything bad happen to me.

And just like that, we're friends again—at least in my mind. I snuggle my nose into the crook of his neck, and a tug pulls at me. Something stronger than friendship. A need, a belonging so primal that I don't know how to process the overwhelming sense of *right*. Perhaps it's a shifter thing.

Carrying me as though I'm the most precious armful in the world, he moves with a graceful strength. So maybe those all-consuming emotions tying me to him got triggered by the lion in him. Maybe it's a cat thing.

He gives me a slow, heart-melting smile. Or maybe it's a Chase thing.

The locker room for the House of Furies feels like a spa complete with a whirlpool, sauna, and massage room. I've cleaned locker rooms before where the stench of unwashed clothes and bodies has near knocked me down. This space smells clean and herbal, the menthol mintiness of eucalyptus oil coming from the mini fridge. Yep, a refrigerator just to chill some scented towels for fragile Furies. I let fresh hints of peppermint and citrus wrap around me, smoothing the edges of my pain.

Until Chase stops suddenly, and my sisters unleash their wings with a *whoosh*.

"What's going on?" I ask, not able to see around the wall that has become feathers and razor-sharp silver edges.

Chase's muscles tense as if he's preparing for an ambush, his breath coming faster against my hair, but neither Kiva nor Sadie glances his way. No, the threat's not one of us. It's something *in* the locker room.

He moves forward, tightening his grip on me, and I can see the note stuck to my locker's steel door, the white of the paper standing out—stark emptiness compared to the jagged scrawl of blood red.

*Take one of mine, and I take one of yours.*
*This is far from over.*

# 8

## CHASE

My lion wants to claw out of my human skin to hunt whoever torments Dottie even in her new form. The note dangles from the locker that has *Rookie* printed in black marker bubble letters on a pink sticky. Whoever left the threat broke in here and targeted her. Not that the locker room is guarded during a practice. No one fucks with Furies. They might not be immortal, but they're hard to kill. Where the Muses might be spotlight stealers and the Nymphs known for sex appeal, my girl's crew earned their fighting reputation.

Dottie has gone still in my arms, her gaze pinned to that damn note. Her scent screams fear and anger. Good, she'll need both if this maniac comes for her again. Not that she will face whatever's coming by herself. I need something to hunt, to stalk, to kill before anything else happens to her.

Kiva curls her wings as though she keeps those dagger sharp edges coiled and ready to strike. In an instant, I realize she's protecting her sisters—Sadie and Dottie—as much as herself. As most shifters would put pack first. I'd never thought of the Fury triads as more than fighting units. "Anyone's senses firing off with an immediate danger?" she asks.

Inhaling, I let the lion sift through the scents. "No. There's a lingering trace of not-quite-human blood, but not Dottie's."

"She's not human anymore." Sadie clutches her whip's handle as though she can beat down any danger.

"I know that." Gods, I'm not an idiot. I speak to Dottie, ignoring her sisters for a second. "Your fresh injuries smell Fury. The red ink smells like human blood—"

"Whose?" Sadie interrupts.

If she thinks I'm about to go bloodhound and sniff the sheet of paper like a cartoon dog for her, she's out of her mind. "I'm a lion, not a damn dog. Being able to determine who, when, or how from a drop of blood or someone's piss? Not in my skill set."

Kiva rips the note off the locker. "This says they'll take one of ours. What's that supposed to mean? One of the Furies?" She sounds as though the idea is laughable. "Someone from another House? Or someone who's important to one of us?"

"Stating the obvious, but none of those could be good." Sadie shudders, and her wings rustle like the pages of a blood-stained grimoire, black with a red sheen highlighting symbols that flicker like a cracked holo-screen. "Let's give the threat to Coach, grab the salve, and get Dottie back to Fury House."

I'm not letting my girl go, not until she's safe. "I'll take you home."

"Chase." Dottie draws out my name until it stretches two syllables long, the way she did when she'd talk me down from a fight at school. "This isn't Petunia—no cops to call and report this to, no cars to drive unless you count the Nymphs' hover-shuttle to the pleasure district. You can't very well carry me the whole way."

"I can, and I would. Shifter strength and speed, remember?" My lion preens a bit, ready to show off how well we could protect her, take care of her if she'd let us.

"While that's really kind, we can manage. Coach will know what to do."

Her rejection—regardless of how sweetly she says it—stings

both me and my beast. "But you don't have your weapon or your wings."

"Put. Me. Down." She bites off each word, and I know my pride has cost me by latching on to her self-doubt, worries she'd shared privately with me. No matter how true my point might've been.

My lion paces in a corner of my mind, snapping at me to make her happy again, to have her rubbing herself against me in contentment again, to not be such a stupid two-legged. "I shouldn't have said that."

"No, you shouldn't have." She has claws of her own, sharp and mean verbal daggers. Maybe she doesn't need a weapon. Maybe she could just tear a man apart with her words. Or maybe that would only work on me. But oh, it does.

I hurt because she's hurt, and now, I've made things worse. *Don't hurt our mate*, the lion grumbles.

*Mate.*

With my beast screaming at my overthinking brain to get out of the way of instinctive need, I won't fight him on naming her as mate. He'd know better than me. For years, I've been able to peacefully coexist with my cat. After the battle and bloodshed with my stepfather, I've been careful to hold the balance and not lose control. My mother's scars serve as a constant reminder to sort through life with both my human and animal natures. But neither side of me can stand to see Dottie scared or suffering. "I didn't mean—"

"Are you going to put me down or you going to assume you know what's best for me? That you know how wings or weapons or anything Fury-related works? Perhaps a shifter girl will shut up and do what she's told for her big, bad alpha cat, but not me."

"Hold up. Most shifter females would crazy-claw the face of any fool who thought he could boss them around, and lions? Women lead our prides, if we belong to one." But my cat's vanity rolls in her praise as I think about what she said. "You think I'm a big, bad alpha?"

"Okay, boyfriend, we'll get her home." Kiva points to a bench. "Put her down before more stupid shit falls out of your mouth."

I settle Dottie on the bench, doing my best not to bump her new injuries or her old ones. Still, she pulls a pained face, and I want to snatch her into my arms again, but I don't. I won't. Not this time anyway. "I'll come by later to check on you."

She nods, not meeting my gaze or saying anything, which means she's hurting. Dottie doesn't hold grudges, doesn't do the silent treatment. She'd rather snap and be sassy, and if she has any fault, it's that she's too sweet too soon to those who mistreat her. Like she's forgiven her momma a hundred times a day for all the years I've known her. Like I'm asking her to excuse me for not doing her the courtesy of letting her know where I've been since I left Petunia, for assuming I knew what was best for her. The realization sobers me, and I leave before I cause her any more pain.

Stumbling through no-thoughts-necessary motions of checking on the bar stock and staying the hell out of their way, I wait until Dottie and her new sisters talk to Coach. Even with shifter hearing, I can't hear what's being said, but Kiva and Sadie, her new family, close ranks—physically and emotionally, based on what I've seen—and the Furies clear out. Dottie leans against her sisters, looking at Coach like the woman could and would shoot out the moon for her Furies. I'm happy she's found people she counts on. But I wish she would count on me.

No matter what I told Sadie earlier, I tear apart the locker room, sniffing the place inch by inch searching for clues, but the not-quite-human male is the only outlier. The wasted hour spent hoping for something to lead me to the killer doesn't do anything to help. I wish I could come up with something to keep my mate safe, to make her want me the way my lion and I both want her.

Still snarling at my failures, I head home and feed the temper, not able to shake the what-ifs. The holo-screen chimes, and I almost don't tap the screen to accept the video message, but I don't need another woman pissed off at me.

I do my best to paste on a smile and work up a pleasant tone instead of the growl stuck in my throat. "Hi, Ma."

"You look like someone drenched your fur in skunk water." Leave it to Ma to cut to the point with Southern mountain lion humor. "What's wrong, baby boy?"

"I've gotten tangled up in an investigation for the Furies."

"You don't normally get ruffled over House business, especially not with those she-devils. Want to talk about what's really bothering you, or do I have to go full curious cat, momma mode to pry the answer out of you? I don't mind interrogating you, but you might not like how it ends."

No, I won't. My Ma can't leave anything alone. If I make her work for information, she won't stop until she's dug up more than I ever wanted to share. "There's a Fury—"

"I knew it. I haven't seen you this messed up and crazy about a girl since sweet Dottie back in Petunia. Tell me about your lady love."

"Well, Dottie's the Fury."

"Oh...oh dear." Her golden eyes widen, her cat flashing in her gaze as if she's ready to pin me with a paw until I explain how my teenage crush is dead and alive again in Syn City. "Let me grab the catnip tea I brewed, and you can fill me in." She leaves and hurries back, a "Cats Rule, Dogs Drool" mug I bought her for her birthday a few years ago cradled in her hands, steam rising to fog her image for a millisecond before the holo-screen adjusts. "Tell me everything."

So I do. From my failure to track the killer to my worries about my stepfather's family finding out where I am. From how we're pretty sure the killer's not a shifter to who knows what's going on with unsolved shifter murders in recent years. From Dottie learning what I am to my belief we could be mates. From the horrible things she has suffered during training to the stupid crap that fell out of my mouth earlier. How Dottie's mad at me. But I don't mention how knowing I hurt her feelings tears me up inside because while talking facts might be easy, talking feelings comes harder.

"Chase Malone." Ma uses my full name in a put-upon voice.

"Yeah, I screwed up." So many times in the last few weeks. For years, I've managed to plod along with my head down, staying clear of any trouble. Dottie shows up, and I become a lion trying to cross a field of eggshells without breaking any while wearing giant clodhopper boots on my paws. My normal grace in making sure I keep to the high hunting ground shattered the moment she came back into my life. "I'm honestly not sure what to do next."

"What's your heart telling you?"

"That Dottie's gone through enough grief with losing her normal life and being shoved into a new one for me to go and add being crazy about her to the heavy load of problems already weighing her down."

"Because you know what's best for her?" No one could miss the trap in Ma's question, loaded and ready to spring.

"No, but I..."

"But you're the big, bad alpha cat who makes assumptions he ought not since I taught you better."

"I thought—"

"You think too much, which is most of the problem, letting your human side make all the decisions without listening to your lion. I didn't ask you what your brain's been telling you. I asked about your heart. What's your lion say?"

"She's our mate, and we should convince her to let us claim and protect her, but I'm doing that by—"

"By making her choices for her? Like you did when we had to leave town? I told you to find her after we left Petunia, but nooo, you had to take her choice away then too. She could've handled the truth about you. She's a tough girl and doesn't need shielding from secrets."

"She died."

"For something that has nothing to do with you. Now, she's a Fury, so maybe *she* should be the one looking out for *you*. You have fangs and claws, but she runs on vengeance and has a pack of trained killers to call sisters. Stop treating her like a fragile friggin' flower, and give her the choice. What's the worst that could happen?"

My stomach churns, a sour sickness burning in my gut. "She could reject me as her mate." Saying the words aloud, no matter how quietly, scares the shit out of me.

"Maybe. But you're already doing that for her by not being honest with her. Right now, you're not protecting her, you're protecting you from facing your fears. I didn't bring up a cowardly lion. No, I raised you better."

Ma's words smack at me, a *bad kitty* rolled-up newspaper to my lion nose. I want to argue, but what if she's right? What if I could be fighting alongside Dottie instead of fighting with her? What if she's been handling the enormous change the best she can, and I've been the idiot dragging her down instead of lifting her up? "I gotta go, Ma."

"Oh?"

"I need to see Dottie."

"Finally, you say something sensible. Good luck." After our *love you*s, I'm out the door and running toward the House of Furies, stopping only to pick up Dottie's favorite flowers and junk food. Or at least these used to be her favorites. I want to learn her new favorites, to know what changed in her old life, to know how I can fit in her new one.

Unsheathing my claws, I dig into the huge tree that serves as the house's home base and climb.

A *whoosh* fills my ears, and a Fury lands on a nearby limb. Sadie walks the skinny branch like she's an Olympic gymnast about to score the gold. "What're you doing here, cat?"

"I'm not here for you. I came to talk to Dottie."

"She's found nothing but trouble in Syn City. Kiva and I didn't like our old third, but Dottie's different." Sadie's expression flickers from confused to determined. "She's nice and sweet. It sounds like you ditched her during her first life, and she deserves better than you making her second life miserable."

"I'm here to apologize to her, and no offense, but whether or not she forgives me—that's up to her."

She eyes me as if she can use her kitchen witchery to stare into me. "Don't hurt her. Or you'll answer to us."

"I won't."

A puff of air, a noise of *yeah-right* disbelief escapes her. "You can say you don't mean to, but you're a shifter. Violence and death follow y'all around. Maybe she came here as your mate looking for you without knowing it. Maybe you followed her that night for the same reason. But she still ended up dead. Remember the Fates with their destiny bullshit play as dirty as the original Furies, but without our code that binds us to serving righteous vengeance."

"If she's my mate, I'll die protecting her. That's the way of shifters."

She looks sad. Gone is the pretentious, uppity act she usually pulls. "Yeah, but nothing—not even you dying—would bring her back a second time around. As you said, it's her call." Straightening with her wings outstretched, Sadie pushes up into the air. "I'll have her meet you on the porch."

Climbing up to the front door fifty feet above the ground, I take a seat on the massive deck with no rails so my feet dangle over the edge. Sadie may have called this a porch, but it's more like a wooden take-off and landing strip for Furies. Except Dottie can't fly, not yet anyway. But she will, and I need her to see how awesome she's always been as well as the potential she has for *more*. More with me if I'm lucky.

A few minutes later, the door opens, not making a single creak but letting the blasting lyrics of a rock party anthem, the *clunk, clunk* of tossed weapons, and loud female laughter escape out into the night air. I'm on my feet in an instant.

"Hiya, Chase." Dottie looks so sexy in cut-off jean shorts and a black top that has silver flowers around the neckline. Her brown hair hangs loose, golden highlights glinting in the porch light behind her. "Nice flowers." She stares at the daisies in my fist.

"I brought them for you. And these." I hold out strawberry hard candies and now-squished cupcakes. "Oops."

"All my favorites." She grins like she did the first day I met her back in sixth grade when she told me we were going to be friends, a sunshine smile.

I swallow past the sudden swell of emotions. "How are you feeling?"

"Better," she says with such conviction that I believe her.

"Sorry about earlier. I let the threat rattle me and my pride get the best of me, but I shouldn't have taken any of that out on you."

She sets her presents on a small, scarred table and sits where I'd been earlier. Swinging her bare feet over the side, she glances up at me. "Don't tell me to be careful. If I fall—which not even I'm that clumsy—you'll catch me, right?"

"Sure." I'd always catch her, but it'd be easier if she'd let me instead of fighting me. "Mind if I join you or are you planning to push me off the porch?"

She pats the place next to her. "Guess you'll have to take your chances."

I wait until we're both staring off toward the lights of the pleasure district, not wanting to spoil this moment of peace between us, but not able to stay silent anymore. "Why'd you come to The Rink that night, Dot?"

"I don't know." There's truth in her tone, none of the pretend B.S. other people might fake. "I wanted to check the city out for Connie to convince her not to come."

"Your little cousin Connie?"

"She's not so little anymore, fifteen going on thirty-five or just plain five depending on the day. Yeah, she loves the Furies, and she's excited I am one. Messaging her has been some of the best parts of my time here so far, and I've gotten her to agree to hold off coming to visit until things calm down."

"You didn't tell her how you became a Fury, did you? She must be worried sick."

"No, I didn't. Normal people don't know that you've got to die first so I left that part out."

"She the only reason you came to Syn City?"

She stares at me, a serious expression bordering on suspicion. "What are you playing at, Chase?"

I take a deep breath. *Here goes nothing.* "I think you came here for the same reason that I've thought about calling you a hundred times every day since we've been apart. We're mates."

"Don't tell me you're buying into the Fury theory on that? Wouldn't we have known when we were younger?"

"We couldn't have done much about our bond at fifteen, and who knows, maybe we did feel something. Since the day we met, I always wanted to be around you, to make you laugh, to listen to you talk. Didn't you feel the same?"

"I did but that doesn't mean we're mates."

"Then how would you explain it?"

"Friendship."

"So a kiss between us as old friends would be just that? No chemistry? No spark? No need for a second one since the first will be more than enough?" She hesitates, and I pounce on the pause. "You want to prove we aren't mates?"

Her gaze slips to my mouth, and her scent goes potent with arousal.

The lion stretches smug and satisfied within me, but I'm wired like I'm coming off a three-day drug bender with the Mad Maes. I've imagined kissing Dottie North for as long as I can remember, the slide of her skin under my hands, the softness of her lips against mine, the sweetness of a pretty girl who grew into a gorgeous woman. But if I want to convince her, I need to make sure this is a bet she thinks she can win and walk away from, a dare she won't refuse. "What do you have to lose?"

"All right," she says, hiking her chin up as though she's a badass challenging me to a fight. "You're on."

I kiss her, taste her for the first time, and suddenly, I know that while she may have nothing to lose, I have *everything*.

# 9

# DOTTIE

CHASE MALONE'S KISSING ME. HIS MOUTH'S ON MINE, HARD BUT inviting, playful even. My brain stops, and my world spins until I lean into him, sure he must feel my heart pounding so hard when I'm pressed against him. He tastes of a wild sweetness like the ripe berries we used to pick off the vines in summertime, and I want this to go on forever. But he stops, and I make an embarrassing whimper of need that I wish I could take back. Except he nips at me again, a teasing snap of his teeth ending in a growl.

"You're such a cat." I swat at him. Two can play at his tricks.

"Guilty." He curves his mouth in a lazy feline grin that shouldn't be so darn sexy. "Still convinced we're just friends?"

"I don't know." I resist the urge to lick my lips, to check if his taste's still there. Nine years ago, I would have fallen over him—or my own feet to get to him—for a chance at another hug or kiss or anything. But now, I'm a Fury who's been left behind once, and I'm not risking him doing it again in my second life. "I mean the kiss was nice..."

"Nice?" He stretches the word, breaking it down like a lion biting back a snarl.

"Don't get all het up about it. I'm sure you—"

His mouth comes down on mine, hot and demanding but still slow and smooth as if he has years to change my mind. Or maybe he's a big cat on the prowl, ready to stalk me as long as it takes for me to agree we might be more than friends. A pulse of power rips through me, something fierce and feral pulling at my chest, a firework exploding from within, tearing me into a thousand shiny, sparkly pieces only to stitch them back together in a beautiful constellation of memories.

Memories with Chase.

I suck in a breath, scrambling to make sense of what just happened. My heart pitter-patters like a hummingbird's wings in a frantic beat, and my every nerve snaps to attention, more alert than the tin soldiers in one of Chase's old games. I stare at him, and he looks as dumbfounded and dazed as me. Only he's surrounded by a crackling rainbow.

Honeysuckle yellow, kudzu green, summer sky blue, muscadine purple, and magnolia white—those colors swirl and spin, a stirring memory of the glowing water globe he once found us that I loved to shake, then wait until the confetti settled, only to shake it again. "Chase, what's happening?"

"The mating bond, I think."

"You don't know?"

A buzz of hornet red flashes across him. "It's not like I've done this before. Mountain lions don't have a group chat. I don't know anyone who has gone through the mating process."

"Your mother?"

"Nope. True mountain lion female. Can't stand anyone but her kid, and she loves me more long-distance."

"What about your dad? Your stepdad?" Although neither man had been in his life very long.

"Strong lions Ma allowed to stay as a defense system, sort of a mandatory, shifter-style home security that came with pride political alliances." A shudder of green-grey flickers in the colors around him, the sickly color of a stormy sky right before a tornado. *Worry.* The realization bats at me as though his lion is pawing to get my attention. Those shades surrounding him ripple with emotions that I can read the same as one of those empaths in the Witching War histories.

"Why are you worried?" I ask him. "I was kidding when I said the kiss only rated nice."

"Why am I worried?" His voice turns mocking, yet he touches me as though I'm delicate, spun sugar. "Someone killed you, and they're out there now taunting that they'll do more. Maybe do worse." Red takes over again. *Anger.*

"You're lying. Not about my murderer, but that's not what you were thinking about. Does your worry have to do with your stepfather?"

"Maybe."

*Definitely* if I'm reading his emotions right. "What about him?"

He looks at the ground, taking his time as if deciding whether or not to tell me everything.

"The truth, Chase."

"I killed him," he whispers. "Not on purpose. He clawed Ma, and I shoved him away from her. His head caught on the kitchen counter, and he didn't get back up. Ma and I left Petunia for good an hour later."

The air rushes out of me. The death had been accidental but so very violent. His stepdad had been an awful, abusive man. I can't imagine how scared Chase must've felt as a fifteen-year-old kid coming into his full powers. Coming into mine as an adult has been terrifying. To add his stepfather's cruelty and his mother's pain and what happened when Chase defended her?

No wonder he ran.

No wonder he didn't come looking for me.

No wonder he hasn't wanted to confess all that happened the night he left.

Until now. Whatever has made him decide to tell me, I grab

onto it. I will sort through the rest of what he told me later, and the past can stay in the past, but I'm not letting him shut me out again in the future. "All right, but what happened between you and him doesn't have to matter now when it comes to us."

"Doesn't it? How can what I did *not* change any long-term future you could see with me as your mate?"

I choose my words carefully. "You said he went after your mom."

"Yeah, he almost blinded her, left her scarred all down one side."

"I'm a Fury. It's my new gig to 'smite' wrong-doers, and maybe your stepdad would've been someone marked for Fury vengeance. I don't know, Chase, but I'd be the pot calling the cauldron black if I judged you for something I swore a blood oath to do for a deity. You're still throwing off worry vibes everywhere when you mention the man, so talk."

"The unsolved shifter murders, I don't think they're tied in with what's happening now."

"How do you know?" Because I'm done accepting assumptions and conclusions from anyone these days when it comes to a killer.

"Those deaths didn't target humans, didn't pose victims as House members, and they didn't involve something so crude as a hammer. No, those shifters died by pinpoint hits designed to kill and then dirtied up to look like another shifter committed the murders."

"Not like the serial killer that Coach described."

"No."

"But if the killer's not coming after shifters, then that doesn't explain your worry."

"I killed my stepfather—"

I'm so frustrated and tired of not getting straight answers from everyone that I can't help but interrupt. "You just described an act of self-defense to protect your mother. People would understand."

"Humans maybe, but the justice system isn't the same with shifters. Most of us follow the law of the marshals—"

I hold up a hand. "I thought the marshals governed *all* shifters, not just the wolves who make up the agency."

"The wolves would like to boss us all around. Truth is they're the only ones with sufficient rank-and-file order to organize a force big enough to impose *any* laws across shifter species, but cougar prides can demand their own payment for the taking of a life. The alpha female of his pride could demand my life in exchange for his."

"That's barbaric."

"It's the shifter way. Now you know why I hid. Investigating the killer here, if the trail links to shifter ties—which I don't think it will—then it could lead his family to me."

"You can't risk that." Not if it means risking him.

"I promised the original Fury that I'd find your killer, and I will, no matter what. But you need to know because the mating bond means you'd grieve more keenly."

"I'm not scared." For the first time of either of my lives. "We can get through this."

"We?"

"Yeah." Confusion threaded with anger wraps around me. "You're the one who said we're mated. Or was that just long enough to steal a couple of kisses and joke's on me when you take off again?"

"No." Golden light as sweet as Tupelo honey spins from him, chasing away my temper. *Love.*

I can't be reading him right, except there's no other explanation. "You love me?" I don't hide the doubt in my voice, couldn't even if I wanted to. Pinning him with a look, I dare him to try and lie. I'll catch him, no doubt.

"Hell, Dottie, how could you ask me that?" He shakes his

head, his too-long hair falling in his face, and my palms itch to push it back. "Why do you think I climbed down the bridge in seventh grade when you dropped your hair thing, the one with the glitter marbles? Or why I ran through fire ants to get your favorite beach ball when it floated away? Or let you almost kill me with a bottle rocket as part of your science project?"

"I'm a klutz, and you were always looking out for me?" Because I don't know if I'm ready for more than that. The kiss had been a test, and this forever-mates-shebang was oh so much more than I'd bargained for, but I don't want to miss out on the chance of loving Chase either. Jupiter's jollies, my heart jumps into my throat, my stomach turns cartwheels, and I wish he'd kiss me so I can't think.

But he doesn't. He stares off into the distance toward the water and bullfrogs and sea hags. "Dottie Mae North, I've loved you from the day we met. I just wasn't smart enough to figure it out until I lost you."

My world narrows to pinpricks of darkness with only the golden light of love curling around me like a lazy cat looking for a pet. I can't see, can't hear past the rush of blood in my head. For years, I dreamed of him saying something a fraction so beautiful. For years, I fantasized of finding him. But this is my second life, and I need to be sure before I promise it to someone else. I already have the Furies carving a claim out of my return with their demands of roller derby and revenge. "I—"

"You don't need to say anything." He traces his thumb over the inside of my wrist like he did the year before he left—our own secret code, he'd called it. "I'm not going to change how I feel about you. Don't know if I could with the bond between us, but I wouldn't want to. Shifter mating relies on both of us accepting a forever together. Otherwise, this connection will slowly fade away."

Wrapping his words around me, I savor the sweetness until I taste the bitterness of that last statement. "You're lying."

"I'm telling you what you need to hear."

"But why—"

"Because I can't lose you again." His voice roughens into a snarl, yet his touch stays gentle. "Not physically. Not emotionally. Not in any way. Leaving you behind in Petunia, not reaching out to you? I thought I did what was best for you."

"Well, thank you for deciding on my behalf." Sarcasm trips off my tongue like a brutal *bless your heart*. "Can't have me thinking for myself after all."

He smiles, and sex appeal rolls off the man. "Ma's already ripped into me for being as dumb as a damn dog. Go ahead. I deserve double of whatever you dish out."

"Well, I can't now." I'm so dang mad that my *can't* rhymes with *paint*. "It's no fun telling you off if you're already grinning like a possum scrounging a spam sandwich." Now he's laughing, and I can't stay irritated with him. I shove at him, and he plummets over the side to the ground oh-so-far below.

My heart stops, my tummy tornado-spins, and my lungs conk out worse than Momma's old clunker. I shriek, scrambling for the edge and overcoming the sick making its way up my throat when the same seductive laugh hits me. Peering over the crooked, creaking slats, I stare the loooong way down. Darkness and silence greet me.

"Chase?" My voice sounds little, like after someone told four-year-old me that the Tooth Fairy was actually a horrible monster who wore the teeth of children around his neck into battle, not caring if the kid lost the tooth naturally...or not.

"Down here, Dot." He hangs by his fingernails from the tree bark. No, not fingernails. Claws. He's still in mostly human form, but he's jammed claws into the wood like he's picking his way along an ice-covered rock face with an ax. "I'm a shifter and a lion. You'd have to push me a whole lot harder to make me fall, and I'd still end up landing on my paws. Or claws."

"That's not funny. For a second, I thought you'd died. Do you have any idea what that feels like?"

"I do." Gone is his smile when he climbs to sit beside me. "Gods, when I found you lying on the path, bloodied and your heart not beating, I felt as though I'd been torn apart from the inside. I would've done anything for another moment with you. So you take all the time you need to decide what to do about us. I'll be here waiting."

With his words, the anger and hurt I've been lugging around for years fizzles into a weight I don't need to carry in this life. Much like the stress of my Momma hounding me for my next paycheck might no longer be a worry with the Furies sending her a steady allowance. Those aren't struggles that'll *poof*, disappear with the wave of some wish-granting wand, but they ease me enough I can breathe.

"I'd better go inside," I tell him. "They're bound to have heard me scream, and knowing Kiva and Sadie, they'll be pressed against the window checking on me."

"Half the house has been watching us the last couple of minutes." He taps his nose. "Can't hide from shifters."

"Ugh, I went from wishing Connie could be my one little sister to having fifty of them, all nosy."

"Can I see you again?"

I'm moving to stand but stop at the vulnerability in his voice. "No more pretending to plummet to your death?" I remember a tiny lizard he once hid in my lunch box and make sure I'm clearer than ghost gin. "None of your pranks or tricks?"

"I promise—proper courting with more flowers and candies and cupcakes."

"You don't—"

"Let me feed you. It's a shifter thing. With most lions? Not so much. Gods know we aren't nearly as bad as bears. But I enjoy watching you indulge in your favorites."

Will I ever get used to my new life? *Our* new life? "All right."

He brushes his lips against mine, a kiss so quick and sweet that I consider asking him to skip ahead of the dating to the dirty parts of mating. But no, I need time to process. I rush inside with the presents he brought and shut the door before I can change my mind, ignoring the pleas from my sisters to share every detail. Later, I stare at the daisies and touch my lips, the taste of lion still on my tongue.

I just need time.

Except time to think is a luxury that a rookie Fury—not even one with a badass nickname—can be allowed. I spend my days with Coach and my sisters, going through roller derby plays and practicing speed skating forward, backward, and sideways until I swear I spin in my sleep. The calendar ticks down to the faceoff between the Furies and the Nymphs, on the sixth of the month. My wings and weapon refuse to make themselves known even with the countdown to the next kill winding closer and closer. Without wings, I don't get to fly in the Witching Wars reenactment or the laser-show fun.

"Have patience. Both your wings and your weapon to call will come," Coach assures me with an easy, infectious confidence. "When the time's right. For now, concentrate on skating. Tonight's bout with the Nymphs will be your debut. You're our starting jammer so slap that star on your helmet, break through the pack, and leave your speed on the rink. I want to see flames sparking from your wheels when you pass everyone up and earn us a point. You got it?"

"Yes, ma'am." I adore Coach. She's the mentor, big sister, and surrogate momma we all wish for. "I'll do you proud. Promise." Waving once last time, she leaves with the other Furies toward the pre-show hype, and I'm stuck by myself.

Well, not entirely alone.

No, armed security guards wait with me in the hallway outside the locker room—a precaution for The Rink deemed necessary after my death exactly one month ago today.

"Dottie?" A high-pitch shriek ricochets off the cement walls and pipes overhead.

I spin on my skates, my heart jumping into my throat, my brain banging out *"the sixth, it's the sixth of the month"* on repeat like a bad drum beat on a staticky station.

Who could've gotten past shifter guards? Except I recognize the rainbow of neon coming my way.

# 10

## DOTTIE

"SO YOU'RE THE NEW FURY EVERYONE'S MAKING A FUSS ABOUT?" A giggling voice turns the question into a lyric. It's the Nymph I met on the first night, her blue and green hair glimmering like an opal beneath the fluorescent lights. *Naughty* shimmers in turquoise sequins on her shirt. Her neon green skates with bright blue wheels gleam iridescent, strapped with prism tape that refracts light in shiny rainbows. She comes in for a hug as though we've been forever besties, glaring at the guards until they back off. "Being a Fury more than suits you. Guess you figured out who you wanted to become."

"Thanks, uh..." I can't remember if she told me her name.

"Neda. No more nosebleed section seats for you, which is fabulous. You deserve some spotlight." She shoots me a sly look. "Do I smell lion on you? Maybe a certain shifter bartender?" Not giving me time to answer, she lets out a happy little squeal. "Oh, but that's wonderful. He's been such a challenge for us Nymphs to figure out, flirty but not available. No wonder if he was waiting for you to arrive as his mate." Her tone sounds as though hearts should flutter around her.

"I—"

"Doll Deadly they're calling you on the Rink like when I called you doll because you're so cute you could be one? I thought it might be you, but you can never be sure with how glam they make us get for the promo shots."

Ugh, I hated the photo shoot. Wearing ten pounds of makeup with painted-on freckles, they'd played up the "doll" aspect like some hot horror show where the Furies always win. "I'm still not used to the name."

"Please, we are the ultimate characters in every human's fantasies. Oh, and most supernaturals' dreams too. Play that up." She flips her hair. "I know I do. Ooh, nice skates."

The wobbly squeak of a handcart echoes along the hall, and Marty peeks out from behind a tower of boxes, his hair dusted with a sprinkle of glittery confetti.

"Ooh, Marty." Neda calls with a pretty trill. "Can you get me some wheels like Dottie's?" She walks away with him, waving over her shoulder at me. "Do they come in neon purple?" she asks him. "Maybe something sparkly?"

He glances back at me, mouthing *told you so* with a grin. I swallow a laugh, my bubbling nerves making me giddy instead of nauseous for a change. Maybe Neda and I could be good friends in this weird world of deity daughters.

"What's up, my Doll Deadly?" Kiva wiggles her fingers in a settle-down motion at a trigger-happy guard.

"Neda stopped to say hi. She's a Nymph," I add when my roommate stares at me like she has no clue who that might be.

"Oh, Naughty Neda. She's fun on the rink, giving out winks to the crowd more than she actually tries to skate derby. You holding up okay? In a few minutes, it'll be time for your big debut."

Thinking about my debut sets off acidic firecrackers in my belly so I change the subject. "You should be at the pre-show. Don't you fly during the reenactments?"

"Nah, Sadie's covering for our triad. Plus, she did some signings while we wait for your trading cards to come in with the new headshots."

I shake my head. "Neda mentioned those. Do we have to do signings and trading cards?"

"Yep, part of the derby gig. Besides, a certain lion will dig you in booty shorts and fishnets with those looong legs."

"Geez, does everyone think we're mates?"

"Everyone *knows* it but you. He's pacing upstairs to come down here and join the guard rotation."

"Don't tell me that he's the reason I have a personal security detail. I should've known when Coach told me to stay with guards the whole night—"

Kiva stops me. "It's the sixth. We all have to be careful. Coach has undercover officers stationed upstairs around The Rink to keep the Furies safe. The other Houses wouldn't go for it, but she tried like hell to get them to. The Syndicate arranged extra patrol for the humans on the paths to the ferry and in the pleasure district."

"What about the path to the bus stop? You know, where..."

"Yeah, I know." She blows out a breath. "Look, some days it's a bitch that I have no idea where I come from, but after seeing you laid out on the trail, I'm glad I don't remember how I died. Coach got them to shut down that path and the bus tonight. She upgraded everyone to a ferry ride for free."

"Coach is the best."

"Totally."

"So the pleasure district? What exactly is it?" Yeah, I've been here weeks and haven't asked out of fear I'd blush to high unholy heavens if I'd guessed right. "Brothels?"

Kiva laughs, the rolling chuckle so much earthier than Neda's giggles. "No. The Syndicate might support selling sexy for derby, but they don't stand for selling people. The pleasure district has casinos, hotels, apartments like the one where your lion lives. Our last third before you came, Janie, retired there from derby to raise her kids and run a crystal shop. Woman makes bank. Nice lady. She couldn't stand me or Sadie. Coach would've split us up if you hadn't come along to make us the triple threat of derby." She flexes her muscles, no less impressive with the elbow pads.

"Dot?" Chase's voice booms along the hall.

"That's my cue," Kiva says, skating away backwards. "Time to roll. See you topside. Knock 'em dead, Doll." She spins and takes off, a guard running after her.

My heart speeds up. It's game time. Then I catch sight of Chase, and my ticker stutter-steps for an even better reason.

His gaze meets mine, and his eyes widen. "Damn, Dot. You look hot...uh, gorgeous...ah, fu—"

"Don't distract me." I skate toward the blaring music and flashing lights of the track, not able to concentrate with him so close.

But he walks next to me, all lazy feline swagger and grace that I wish I could borrow a fraction of. His easy confidence makes me want to speed off and leave his too-handsome self behind. Except he slides a slow, heated glance my way. "You've got this. I'll be watching out for you the whole bout so you can focus on winning. Show everyone who the new derby queen will be."

"Me?" Yeah, not convincing, but I haven't skated into a pole or anything solid in days, so yay for small victories.

"Damn straight, my dangerous mate."

The cheers and applause cut off any answer I can make, and the knowing gleam in his eyes says he timed his parting shot to be sure he'd get the last word. I stew in my "could've, would've, should've" musings for a second, but the view of the packed-to-the-roof Rink from the track has my body jittery, my throat closing up, and my lungs forgetting how to work.

Sadie rolls to a stop in front of me. "Welcome to the show," she yells. "Don't throw up or you'll skate in your own puke. Now move, newb."

Her insult has me pushing forward, shoving down fear and

pulling up speed. Neda waves from across the track before slapping a silly game face on. They're right. These humans came for a show, and we're gonna give them one.

"No prisoners, Furies," Coach hollers. "Annihilate those Nymphs."

We play like we can outrun the killer coming for the tourists. We play as though we can teach him to fear us. We play for us and for the humans who scream our derby names. A few bumps, some new bruises, and a whole lot of sweat later, I score the winning point, and we beat the Nymphs. Barely.

Neda comes in for a quick high five. "I'd hate you, Dottie, but we're gonna be tight. You, me, and your studly shifter." Her giggling cuteness makes it impossible to do anything but smile back. "Gotta score me some sweet skates like those. See you later, Dottie doll." Blowing a kiss, she rolls away.

"Making friends with Neda?" Chase asks from beside me.

I jump to find him so close so fast. "Come to escort me back to the locker room?"

He shakes his head with a grin at a joke I don't get until Furies surround me, whoops and battle cries and a dousing of water and sports drink. Ugh...sooo sticky.

"Time to celebrate," Coach yells, and I'm almost afraid they're about to fly off with me for some weird ritual, only it's time to be congratulated by the crush of humans, which might be more awkward.

I pose with fans for selfies, sign autographs, and pretend I'm Doll Deadly for the tourists. Not someone who was human just like them only weeks ago. My adrenaline dumps in a rush that leaves me weary and wrung out. Any of these humans could be the next victim, and none of them know the danger. The blood-red writing on the threat haunts me. What good is derby with a murderer out there?

"Move out, Furies," Coach calls. "It's closing time." Her good-humored time-to-go gets the few humans left moving toward the exits. The bars and booths on the circle above have been broken down and the workers have almost finished.

According to Chase, they do bare minimum clean up after shows, then the sanitation staff comes in to finish during the day. When I'd asked him if they might need an extra experienced cleaner, if I should apply, he'd laughed at me. But I'd take some good hard labor these days to work through my worries that creep in every minute I'm not skating.

"Keep smiling." Kiva slides next to me. "We'll shower off the grit and head back to the House of Furies. The patrols will keep up rotations all night. We'll take away his targets until we find him."

Breathing past the stink of sweat, I swallow, ignoring my dry throat and the taste of bile on my tongue. The Furies storm the locker room en masse in a flurry of wings, war whoops, and can't-mess-with-us, untouchable cockiness. Steam rolls from the showers to the *clang clang* of gear dropping to metal benches and *whack whack* of lockers being slammed. Excitement and happiness bubbles in the air through the scents of soap and perfumes spritzes, and my mood lifts like a kid's helium balloon climbing toward the top of the bouncy castle.

By the time I come out of the locker room to see my lion lounging like he doesn't have anywhere else in the world he'd rather be, I loop my arm through his and lay my head on his shoulder. "Thanks for sticking around while we showered off the yuck."

"I'll always wait for my mate, even when she doesn't call me hers yet." The tenderness in his voice and the beaming happiness of his emotions wrap around me, and I can't even be mad about him subtly pushing me on the mate thing.

"Come on, you two." Kiva follows Sadie, who'd gotten an armed guard to walk with them toward the track. "Our sister witch likes to thank the track for no injuries, for a good skate. It's a tradition for her."

"Sounds good to me." I would take any of the good woo woo help we could get until we got through this night with no other death.

Chase walks beside me. "We'll catch him, and you're safe tonight. They've hustled the humans to the ferries or hotels. He'll have to search elsewhere for his sick fix."

Sadie's shriek kicks off the hairpin trigger on my fear, my lungs tightening painfully and my upper back burning where the wings inside me beat against my skin for freedom they can't find.

"Stay back," a guard calls. But it's too late. We've already seen.

Lit by a single spotlight, hanging from the center of the pit, dangling from a cord as though she's stilled in flight, a woman's body slumps against the rope tying her upright. Ugly black plastic toy wings have been stuck to her back, the kind they sell for kids to dress up as Furies. It's a horrific imitation of the real thing, crooked and tiny where they jut out from the woman's ripped shirt. But the wings aren't the worst.

No, the blue and green hair covering her hanging head pricks tears in my eyes and burns my skin. The fallen neon skate with prism tape has a sob escaping my raw throat.

*Neda.*

He killed Neda.

*Take one of mine, and I take one of yours.*

*This is far from over.*

Coach had been so careful protecting the Furies and the humans. She'd pushed the Syndicate to protect the Houses. Now he'd taken one of us in the most gruesome display.

"Cut her down," I whisper. "Please don't leave Neda like that."

I've barely gotten the words out of my dry mouth, over the bile coating my tongue, when a security guard rushes forward.

"Doll Deadly?" he calls. The name sounds so foreign, the idea of derby forgotten, the reality of anything so hazy that I don't answer. "Um, ma'am? I found a girl hiding in an AC vent. She says she belongs to you." The massive shifter holds a gun strapped over one shoulder and, using his other arm, pulls a human pitching a hissy fit from behind him.

"Told you," the girl spits and sputters from beneath a mess of brown hair. Her big brown doe eyes shoot fiery temper at the shifter who hangs on to her.

All I can see is blackness with white stars and a slim beam of light around the fighting girl, my cousin, the last person I want in Syn City right now. "Connie, what are you doing here?"

# 11

## CHASE

SEEING A YOUNGER, SCRAPPIER, CURSE-WORD-SLINGING VERSION OF Dottie shakes me out of staring at poor Neda. The Nymph showed up a couple of years ago, her Irish accent so strong that I couldn't understand her drink orders half the time. She'd been a party girl who'd teased that dancing and neon glowsticks could end any fight. No one deserves to die and be displayed in such a brutal way, but especially not fun-loving Neda.

"Dottie, ohmygods." Connie runs her words together as if the teenager is a streaming virtual reporter sped up to double time, her backwoods Petunia twang deepening every second. "That's Naughty Neda. What happened to her? And why're Fury wings stuck to her? Everybody knows she's a Nymph. Who would've hurt Neda?"

The shifter holding her stares at Connie like she's a ticking time bomb, and I pity him. The North women can be a lot to take in when they're calm and at home, talking about school drama and homework. In the middle of a murder scene, Connie is off-the-charts emotional and expressive, waving her arms around while she talks and almost clocking the guy in the head a couple of times.

"Let her go," I say. "She's family." Because with shifters, that explanation covers so much.

He releases his hold, and Connie comes flying into Dottie's arms, gushing something that sounds like crying fangirl exclamations toward Kiva and Sadie. "You guys are my favorite, but somebody killed Neda," the kid says before her words muffle against her cousin's shirt.

"Get the girl out of here," Kiva tells Dottie.

I agree. Witnessing such horror is difficult enough for those of us who already knew a killer stalked Syn City and would be making a move tonight. For a teenager fresh off the ferry here for the first time? It must be even more terrifying. "I'll come check on you both in five minutes," I offer. "That work?"

Dottie nods and leads her cousin up the stairs. They disappear through a side door toward the concourse, flanked by armed guards.

As soon as they're out of sight, Kiva takes wing and checks Neda's body. "She's still warm. Whoever did this killed and displayed her fast. One blow to the back of the head. Looks like he used a hammer. She probably never saw him coming. Any reason I can't bring her down?"

They look to me. "No. Too many human smells to catch a distinct scent in The Rink," I explain. "He's covering his tracks, but he had to be here tonight, had to have access to Neda and the areas closed off to tourists."

"This might be our best chance to catch him," Sadie says.

With Fury strength and speed to rival a shifter's, Kiva gently brings Neda's body to the ground and brushes the Nymph's hair out of her lifeless eyes.

Sadie stays where she is, not moving toward the woman she can't heal. "The Houses will be on full alert. I'm sure one of the guards has already told them. Coach will be waiting for us, Kiva. Come on."

"She was one of us. Not a Fury, but still..." The anger in the other woman's voice shakes with a vengeance the likes I've never heard, one so bitter it'd terrify anyone guilty of this crime.

"I know." Sadie puts a hand on her sister's shoulder. "The Nymphs will mourn her. We'll avenge her." She looks to me. "You vowed to an immortal to find this motherfucker so we can deliver retribution. It's time to keep your promise, cat."

I don't take offense. No one would at the devastation buried beneath the polish. My guess would be she's barely hanging on. I take a deep breath. "That not-quite-human scent I caught in the locker room when we found the threat left for Dottie? It's here. *He's* here. We need to do a full lockdown, check for any supernatural or other humans who might've hidden through The Rink's closing time."

"No other humans." The same shifter who hauled Connie in shakes his head. "The wildcat kid who knew your mate? Only she remained. Everyone else has been gone for half an hour."

"Not everyone," Sadie insists. "You've missed someone, *shifter*." She says the word like it's synonymous with murderer, and I almost forget the pity I had for her.

"The kid didn't do it," Kiva says. "She was scared out of her mind, and she wouldn't have the strength."

The shifter guard raises his hands as if remembering belatedly that while the Furies might be the protected, they should also be the feared.

"I've had eyes on the girl." Vera, a wolf shifter who usually works undercover security at the casinos, clears her throat. "Most teenagers fidget or stay glued to their comms, but not her. She's been in her seat through the whole show, watching the newest Fury. No way anyone could miss the scent of an innocent that fresh. Like a pup rolling in mud for the first time."

"The kid's Dottie's cousin," I say. "Her only family other than her mom."

"Shit." The news seems to stir Kiva beyond her grief. "We'd

better get up there and escort our sister and the girl back to the house."

"I'll come with you." I don't wait for them to agree, sprinting up the stairs, stopping only when I'm around the bend from Dottie. No need frightening Connie any more than she's already been. Except the girl's not scared.

She's babbling faster than a predator shifter chases after an elk steak. "Persephone's—"

"Connie." Dottie cuts in, teacher prim. "You're not supposed to be here. Does your daddy know you came to Syn City?"

"Please, as if my daddy knows anything I do." Connie sounds like the master of eye rolls. She must've swallowed her scared real quick. "He's gone on a three-week haul and left me under the tender mercies of your mother. She said she's been getting your paychecks from a new cleaning gig here, so I asked to come stay with you."

"When Momma was sober?" Dottie's tone says she doesn't hold much hope of that.

"Of course not, cuz." Connie waves a hand. "You sent her money which means she'll be popping painkillers 'til the bottle's empty. Last week, she wasted half of the cash on some sham witch-repellant charm. I left her a note, telling her I'd check on you so she doesn't have to, said you invited me to stay." She glances my way. "Why, hello." The drawl in her voice sounds like a barfly looking to get laid instead of someone still in high school. "Wait, don't I know you?"

"Hiya, Connie, I'm Chase. You were in maybe kindergarten or first grade when I last saw you."

Her eyes go wide and round. "You're Dottie's lost love. Oh my gods, she moons over you." I want her to go on and on because damn, I couldn't have dreamed of my girl missing me, but guilt eats at me. Like Ma said, I could've told Dottie what happened. I could've trusted her to keep my secrets.

"That's enough." Dottie sounds as though she's about to scream.

"Agreed." Coach steps next to her. "We need to move out. You trust your kin with our secrets?" Barely waiting for Dottie to nod, she continues, "Good. You two will travel with us by air. I need triads on patrol in the pleasure district. The rest of you remain on watch. Do not let this killer invade our house, or, if he does, show him how Furies treat those who murder women, humans, Nymphs, the helpless. Yes?"

"Yes, Coach." An angry war shout goes up from dozens of pissed-off fearmonger deity daughters.

"Dottie." I pull her close. "I've got to stay, to see if I can pick up any leads from the scene."

"Okay." She's fighting nausea, judging by the curl to her lips. Her scent has fear edged over her usual sweet.

"You all right?"

"I will be when Connie's safe." Her breathing's shallow, and her pulse hammers so hard that I can hear it over my own. "I need to get her to the House of Furies. Coach says she can bunk with the sisterhood for a few days. By then, I should have convinced her to go home."

"We're calling in every shifter we can find to help. I asked the wolves' marshal service to come, but they won't since the victims aren't shifters, and the Syndicate won't recognize their authority. Coach will get us approval to shutter the businesses in the pleasure district for the night and go door to door checking human visitors. Then we can do a sweep of the staff."

"Why do you have to help?" she asks.

"He killed you, left the note on the locker threatening you. I need to find him. I know I'm just a bartender, but I've got a blood oath to an immortal backing up my claim to be a part of this. I'll stay on top of things. Promise."

Fear radiates off her, and it guts me. "What if I can't keep Connie safe?"

"You will." I need her to believe in herself, but the doubt in her eyes has me rushing to make things better if I can. "*We* will, along with Coach and your sisters."

"What if I got Neda killed? By not understanding that the threat could mean any of the Houses, not only the Furies or humans? By talking to her before the show—"

"You did nothing wrong. He's messing with us, maybe trying to pit the Houses against each other, making our safe places feel scary. Don't let him win."

"With or without my weapon to call, I'll destroy anyone who tries to hurt Connie." Determination and meanness and justice compete in her promise—announcing her as a Fury through and through.

"Now you know how I feel about the person who hurt you." I sweep my fingers through her hair, above the skin that would've been scarred by now if she'd lived through the attack on her. Knowing she's scared, that she has reason to be, infuriates my lion, who doesn't want to leave her alone, but she'll be at the House of Furies, the safest place in Syn City for her to be.

She tips her head to cradle her cheek in my palm, and the tender action undoes me. I'll do anything to protect this woman I've loved as long as I can remember. A golden glow radiates inside me when I think of our mating bond—so shining and bright that my cat bats at the ribbon connecting us with Dottie. But not now. I've got a promise to keep first.

Hours later, I'm exhausted and no closer to the killer. The Furies have arrived to patrol and keep panic from spreading, maintaining order and implementing curfew without calling it one. I've gone through travel records for every tourist on the island, and none of them made the trip exactly one month ago. Other shifters have pulled the logs for everyone who left the island tonight, but the last time I called for an update, they were no closer to a match. Which leaves going door to door through the staff quarters.

Interviewing every single staff member from concession stand workers to janitors to audio-visual techs means slow, painstaking work. To make matters worse, a severe case of food poisoning has hit every staff member who ate the cream-filled pastries in the work lounge tonight, including a couple of guards. We stock up on bottles of electrolyte solution to hand out since the doctor's stuck sedating most of the Nymphs to prevent self-harm.

Those from that House who didn't have to be drugged out of their mind have pieced together a list of anyone they saw talk with Neda tonight, but I might as well interview everyone who'd been on shift. She'd been so friendly, stopping to say hi to most. A name stands out to me—Marty, and not just because my lion's tail has a perma-twitch over the way the guy makes puppy-eyes at my girl. He's worse than a damn wolf sniffing around where he's not welcome.

I pound my fist on his apartment door, and Vera glares at me so hard I wonder if she read my mind on that last thought. Lions, wolves—we're not far off from the cats hating dogs cliché.

"It's not him," she says. "All you predatory males go insane when someone's threatening your mate. Take a breath. Read the scent."

"He's taking too long to answer the door. Maybe he's hiding because he's guilty."

She covers her nose. "Or because he's sick as a friggin' cat drowning in hairballs."

"Ha ha." The door opens, and a whiff of nasty coated in menthol and bleach hits me in the face. "Gods, what died?"

Marty hangs onto the wall like he'll be horizontal in a millisecond if he lets go. His skin's pasty pale, he's sweating, and my cat's betting he'd be clammy if I dared to touch him—which I'm not. "Can I help you?" He sounds as though his question's dragged up and over glass shards.

Vera sends an *I-told-you-so* look my way. Such a know-it-all wolf.

"We need to ask you about tonight, about Neda."

Marty leans his forehead against the doorjamb. "Tell her I ordered the skates in the color she wanted. They should be here before her next practice."

Shit, he doesn't know. I've miscalculated.

Shoving a bottle of electrolyte elixir at him, Vera blurts out, "She's dead."

I barely step aside before Marty dry heaves and drops to the spot where I stood, crumpling to his knees like a puppet whose master dropped his strings.

"She...how..." He coughs, sputters, and my lion wants to snarl in disgust.

Vera pulls a syringe out of her back pocket, twists off the end, and laser injects something into his arm.

"What the hell?" I ask her. "He's telling the truth. Don't poison him."

"Relax." She screws the cap back into place on the syringe. "It's anti-nausea meds coupled with a light sedative so he can rest. Doc gave me a few doses before he headed over to the Nymphs. Have you seen Marty around free food? The man eats like a hyena. He doesn't care what it is or how rotten it might be. If we're lucky, he hit the pastries early tonight. The way he gorges, he would've eaten enough for ten people and saved some others from being sick. Let's get him back inside and make him down the electrolytes."

We finish taking care of a now-sobbing Marty. "Think we should call someone to take care of him?" I ask.

"You ever seen him with anyone longer than five minutes?" She keeps her voice low enough only a shifter could hear her. "I don't think he has any family or real friends to call."

I hate to admit that other than catching him staring at my mate, I haven't spared Marty much thought. He's the proverbial freshman who'd get his head shoved in the chem-toilets by every jock in the school—not smart enough to bribe with homework duty, not ugly enough to mock in public, but scrawny enough he'd have made an easy target. "You need anything?" I ask him, guilt a foreign concept to my lion but far too familiar to me. "Want us to find someone to stay with you?"

His bleak eyes meet mine. "What happened to Neda?"

"She was murdered." I gentle my tone, but there's no softening the truth. Still, better I tell him than Vera the Vulgar Truthsayer over there. "After the show tonight."

"Who would hurt a nice Nymph like Neda?" He asks a good question.

"No one would've had cause." No one without a vicious vendetta against the Houses, but everyone in Syn City owes their allegiance, their paychecks, if not their lives to the Syndicate.

"Let's go," Vera says. "We've got more than thirty other employees to check out."

I grumble a halfhearted wish for Marty to feel better, and we go knock on the next door.

At the end of the interviews, I've got no leads to report to the Furies. How am I going to tell Dottie? I head toward my apartment to shower and change. Maybe I can figure out yet another way to say I've failed by the time I make it to the House of Furies. Except a Fury waits on the balcony of my apartment—three of them, actually. Dottie argues with Sadie, who's working on breaking into my sliding glass door, and Kiva sits with her ankles crossed all ladylike except she's wearing studded leather pants with her legs stretched along the railing. I don't want to know which of them flew Dottie over from the House and up onto my balcony.

"Stop trying to jimmy the door." Dottie's whisper to Sadie whips to my ears like a favorite tune thanks to shifter hearing.

"You wanted to stop by to check on him." The blonde doesn't stop wiggling a screwdriver that's likely from the toolbox I keep on the balcony. Note to self, don't leave shit unlocked even on a fourth-floor apartment when half the city's residents can fly or climb walls. "Although why you want to keep company with a shifter, I'll never understand."

Kiva spots me and does a cutesy wave of her fingers in my direction without saying a word.

"Do you hate all shifters?" my mate asks Sadie. "Or just my boyfriend?"

Well, drop a house on me, Dottie's calling me her boyfriend to her second-life kitchen witch sister. Isn't that the sweetest? I would claw my way up the wall, but there would go my security deposit, so I settle into a crouch and leap to a second-floor balcony two doors down from my place with a thump. Normally, I could go higher and land softer, but I'm exhausted.

"What was that?" Sadie asks.

"No idea," Kiva answers. *Liar.* Another quick leap, and I make it to the railing across from her. "Hiya, kitty cat." She gives me a wicked grin. Add fangs, and the woman could've made an alpha tigress shifter.

"Chase, we were just stopping by..." Dottie sounds like the guilty one when she's the only one who couldn't have flown herself up here. Not unless she's found her wings in the last few hours.

"Breaking in?" I ask Sadie.

The blonde tosses my screwdriver into the strewn mess she's made of my toolbox with a clang. "We told her not to bother with the field trip to your lair, but she wouldn't listen."

Dottie pinches the bridge of her nose. "I can't go anywhere with you two."

I almost feel bad for her—almost—but if she'd come by herself, then I would've had one more worry. With whip-wielding Sadie and hatchet-happy Kiva, she travels with her own personal, messed-up protection detail. "Want to come inside? I could let you in the front door."

"Where's the fun in that?" Kiva asks.

Not answering her question, I jump across to the walkway

and use a key to go inside, opening the balcony door in seconds. Dottie looks so fresh and pretty in that outfit, her hair curled, but her eyes—they're haunted. The need to comfort her overwhelms me even as I calm just breathing in her scent. "How are you holding up, Dot? How's Connie?"

"She's doing okay considering the shock of everything. I should've known she would be better prepared for this life than I was the way she follows the Houses in every gossip column."

Kiva giggles. "Our Coach loves having a Fury fan underfoot who knows our playbook better than we do. She'll make her an assistant before the month's out."

"Connie won't be staying." Dottie snaps out the words like this is part of an ongoing argument that I've interrupted. "I'll hang out here with Chase until he brings me home." She stares at me with those big brown eyes. "If you'll have me." As if I could ever deny her anything, let alone a visit.

"Sure." Now I sound like a lovestruck teenager no older than Connie. "Come on in."

"Alone." She glares at her sisters.

"Later. Comm if you need us," Kiva calls, and Sadie shakes her head. They both drop over the side of the balcony with a *whoosh* of unfurled wings.

I catch a hint of something unfamiliar in Dottie's scent as she watches them go. "What is it, sweetheart?"

"Their wings fly so strong and true. What do you think mine will look like?"

"Perfection."

"You're saying that because you're convinced I'm your mate."

"Still true." Both parts of what she said, but I'm too tired to argue.

She follows me inside, taking in my two-bedroom apartment with a quick glance.

Trying to see what she might, I come up with boring but clean. "I haven't done much decorating." A comfortable couch and chairs in the living room, photos of me and Ma in one small holo-frame, and a short video of Dottie when she was younger than her cousin in another. Of course, she zeroes in on the last.

"You kept this old holo-vid of me?" She sounds stunned. When will she stop doubting how important she is to me?

"It was all I had of you."

"You must've taken these images down the road from your old house, by the blackberry bushes."

"You were laughing. Prettiest girl in Petunia. Or anywhere for that matter."

She looks at me, and some of the sadness fades from her gaze. "You're worn out. Let's get you cleaned up and in bed."

"Only if you'll stay. Otherwise, I'm good." I'm falling asleep on my feet, but no way will I admit that.

"I'll stay."

And she does. She doesn't even comment on the Doll Deadly poster tacked to my bedroom wall that the merchandise manager let me have before they're released for sale because "mates get first dibs." I shower as quickly as I can, scared she'll be gone when I come out, that maybe I imagined her here in an exhaustion-fueled dream. But no, she waits and curls up beside me. I sleep, and still, she stays, and I wake with Dottie's curves pressed against me and her lips on mine. My blood turns to flame.

"This doesn't mean we're mates." Her murmur against my mouth tastes so sweet but stings like venom.

My lion snarls low and vicious in my throat, but I flip her onto her back and nuzzle her neck, slow and gentle as a fucking domesticated kitten with a ball of string attached to a stick of dynamite. "Let's see if I can convince you otherwise."

# 12

## DOTTIE

"Nuh uh, Chase Malone. You keep your kisses to yourself if you're going to insist on this mate thing." Because right now, I'm out of my head drunk on him, and I might say yes. His weight's heavy against me, his scent's scrumptious, and his shifter skin blasts me with heat. "You want me to stay? You play by my rules." His scruff scratches my neck, and his warm breath tickles. "Quit it. You're making me laugh on purpose.

"Making you laugh isn't against the rules...yet." Arrogant cat doesn't even sound sorry.

"Well, it will be." As soon as I come up with some rules and remember how to think enough to give them. "Rule one, my life with the Furies has to come first, over everything. Even a mating bond."

"I knew you would come around—"

"Nope. I'm not agreeing to be mates." Or I don't think I am anyway. "I'm just telling you how it would be if I did. Rule two, this is me using you to forget everything else going on. We clear?"

"I'm good with you using me." He gives me a lazy feline smile, and I swear I hear the sexy snarl drip off every word.

My good sense empties right out of my head. If he asked me

to run away with him and leave our responsibilities and blood vows behind, I might. Nope. I need to focus. He snaps his teeth at me like he's impatient to get started, and the teasing *chomp-chomp* reminds me. "Oh, and last thing, no clawing and no biting. Deal?"

"Yep, but you can feel free not to stick to any of those rules, especially the last." His cockiness needs to be leashed before he and his ego take up all the room in this bed. It's time to remind him that I'm not the same girl from Petunia. Not anymore.

"You sure about letting me have my way with you? I'm Fury strong now. I could make a poor itty bitty kitty cry."

His gaze gleams wicked, and he rolls again. I land on his muscled chest with a little shriek. "Do your worst," he says, daring me to make good on my threats.

Well, shoot. I might've talked big game, but now, I'm the one who's unsure. While he'd been asleep, he'd been so much like the boy I'd given my whole heart to years ago, not knowing that teenaged love could be the lifelong thing. Or two lifetimes now. He's always handsome, but when he sleeps, there's a boyish sweetness to him, a vulnerability that reminds me why I fell for him the first time. His dark blond hair with sun-streaked strands frames a strong jaw and bitable lips. The bitable part was what got me into this in the first place. I'd wanted a taste, so I'd stolen one kiss, then another.

"You're plotting awful loud, Dot." He runs his callused palms over my thighs, and I'm suddenly glad I wore my shortest off-the-skating-rink shorts. "I can almost see the feathers coming outta your ears."

"Cannot. You don't even know if my wings will have feathers."

"True, but we know they'll be beautiful and black."

"What's with the basic black obsession?" I trace lines on his bicep with my fingertip, our initials the same as I wrote in my diary a decade ago.

"Didn't your sisters tell you? The story goes you become granddaughters of Nyx, the goddess of night, when you're turned.

It's why Furies generally fly under the cover of night. Just like the Houses don't allow helicopters or planes here. It's part of the whole mystique package Syn City sells. Besides, can you imagine you trying to dodge some idiot pilot?"

Worry tugs at me. "What if I don't ever find out what my wings look like? What if mine are stuck back there underneath my skin? What if I stay grounded, unable to fly forever like some squawking chicken?"

"Ah hell." Chase comes up into a sit, leaning against the headboard and lifting me as if I weigh nothing before pulling me against him in a rough hug.

Freakin' shifter strength and warmth and smell. I snuggle close and sigh in an epic performance that fifteen-year-old me would've been proud of. "So much for my seducing you." His chuckle rumbles through me, and dang the man, even his laugh is sensual. I kinda hate him except I don't. Not even a little bit. "Why are you laughing at me now?"

"Come on, you felt the mating bond when we kissed. Or, at least, I thought you did."

"Yeah." I'm not confessing more. Not yet anyway. "So?"

"So..." His tone goes intense, searching, as though he's trying to say something without putting it in words. "Read me as best you can through our unfinished bond and see if I'm making fun of you."

Closing my eyes, I listen to his heart beating and sort through the colors radiating off him. The warm gold I've grown accustomed to sensing around him, a strong rainbow of happiness and hope with not a smidge of bad humor. I open my eyes and tip my head back to find him watching me as if he could stay this way for hours. "You're not?" I guess.

He rubs his hand along my shoulder blades. "Nope. Your wings will come. What did the other Furies say about how theirs manifested?" Talking about wings and Furies as if this might be normal pillow talk, he puts me at ease.

"Coach says sometimes strong emotions trigger the first time. Like everything else from finding our weapon to call to going full Fury—whatever that means. The emotional tripwire's why Sadie and Kiva keep trying to frighten me."

"You're from Petunia. You're hard to scare."

"True, but they didn't know me in my first life. Still, I've felt every possible emotion from excitement to victory to terror to... what I felt when we kissed." The memory ignites my craving for him. No matter what else may be bothering me, Chase leaves me tied up in knots of need and want and everything in between.

"Want me to kiss you again and see if that helps with your wings? Or with your devilish plan for seducing me?"

"Diabolical." I've wanted to use that word for years.

"Truly?" He murmurs the question against my lips.

"Mmm hmm." Sure. For my wings. No other reason. Not the heat in my belly or lower.

His mouth on mine is magic more than anything else I've found in Syn City. Forget the Furies and the flying and whatever else I haven't yet learned about the legends come to life in the Houses. His taste is more addictive than the faerie wine the preachers warn of, richer than the bottle of muscadine moonshine we swiped off Momma's shelves and drank ourselves silly on a back country road.

I should've known Chase might be more than human when his body tore through the alcohol faster than any of the racers down at the dirt track. On his lap, straddling him and moving my hips against his, I'm more at home here than I ever felt in Petunia. I don't want to stop because his kisses make me ignore everything else.

When he breaks the kiss, I'm not sure which of us is breathing harder, but his gaze glows golden, and his mountain lion stares back at me through his eyes. "Chase?" My voice comes out smaller, more prey than I'd intended.

"Shit." He rubs his face as if he can wipe away the shifter part of him. "I didn't mean to scare you. I'm not used to this deep of a connection, not one so raw that you can see all of me." He sounds almost angry, snarling and snapping.

I don't bother taking his emotional temperature. No, I snap right back. "As if I'm super experienced at any of this sexy stuff?"

Confusion flashes in his green-again eyes. "What do you mean?"

"Aw, now you've done it. I wasn't going to say anything, but no, you had to ruin my plans of kissing you until we're both naked and having a good time instead of arguing?"

"Who's arguing?"

"You are." Can the arrogant man not hear his growly self?

"Time out. How experienced are you?"

"On a scale of one to ten? I'm batting negative two. Come on, Chase. We grew up in the same small town. It wasn't like I had many choices. You were the only good one, and you up and left me." Now, I'm yelling at a predator shifter while sitting in his lap, which can't be either smart or sexy. "You know what? Never mind. I'll message the House and one of my sisters can—"

"No, please don't go." His voice comes out soft in the charged air between us. He yanks me closer, resting his forehead against mine. "I'll never leave you again. Promise. We don't have to kiss or talk or do anything. Just stay."

"That's not gonna work for me." I pull away, breaking contact long enough to peel my shirt off and toss it somewhere. I don't care where. The only thing I care about is getting skin to skin with my maybe mate. "I'm not here to fight. I want to be with you. Don't you want me too?"

"Badly." His voice goes rough and low, and his gaze travels between mine and my cotton-candy pink bra. "Wow."

Three cheers for having a beauty queen roommate who talked me into blowing way too much of my Fury wardrobe allowance on fancy lingerie. "The panties match," I say, slipping a finger under a strap. The lace slides against my skin, delicate and frilly and outrageously fragile. "Wanna see?"

"I'd rather taste." He moves faster than I can follow, but he's oh so gentle with his kiss trailing along my jaw. "I can smell your arousal, can hear your heart beating faster, can sense your emotions. When the mating bond opens, you slam into me like the softest sledgehammer."

"I do?" My first instinct's to apologize, but he doesn't sound upset.

"You're fury and fierceness, sugar and sweetness, my happiness and my hope. Your smile lights my whole world, and your anger—well, let's just say my cat appreciates your claws. But when you hurt? I can't stand it. You could crush me." Yet, he cups my breast as if he's afraid of breaking me. "Tell me I can taste you. Say yes."

"Yes." I sound confident and powerful and not at all like myself. Or maybe more myself than I've been before. He reaches for my bra, one claw sliding out, but I knock his hand away. "Don't you dare. This is my favorite." I hurry to unhook the fancy lingerie and shimmy out of the lace.

"Might as well take off everything else unless you want to risk your cute outfit." He flexes his fingers—very human fingers for now, but I've seen how fast he can unleash those claws. "Shredding accidents happen."

"You wouldn't. These clothes were expensive."

"I'll buy you new ones."

I poke at his chest with my fingernail that's stubby compared to what he's hiding. "I said no clawing." But my fussing has no fight, and I forget about shyness because he has his mouth on my skin, at my throat and working his way down my naked body as he slips further onto the bed, holding me up, not allowing me to fall or to follow him. I need to be closer, to feel him skin to skin. Unintelligible sounds come from me—whispers and promises and sighs. But no, he just pins me there, my knees sinking into the soft mattress, the heat of his body and his lips making me melt. "Chase..."

"I could spend an entire night licking you." He punctuates his words with kisses that leave trails of fire in their wake, my body coming alive with demands of *more* under his touch. "Bury my face between your thighs and bring you to tears so I can lap up your orgasm on my tongue."

"Yes." I want *that*, my legs tremble with want of that. Barely able to catch a breath, I know he has to hear my heart pounding when he takes my nipple into his mouth and sucks. My body lights up like fireworks, those ribbons of color flowing between us through the mating bond exploding into a riot of gold and silver —curling around us in a tangle that's as much a coming together of the two as a fight to come out on top in some metallic victory that's going to drive me out of my mind. "More, Chase."

With cocky cat arrogance, he slides his face between my thighs, rubbing his scruff against my sensitive skin as if he's marking me with his scent.

"Oh my gods, you... I..." Embarrassment floods me, igniting the tiny slivers of skin he hasn't already set on sensual fire, but he grips my hips to hold me still.

He strokes his fingers *there*, and I come undone. I'm spiraling up, up, up toward the moon, a shooting star flying through the stratosphere with no need for wings. I writhe, the word I never understood in those romance novels Connie has even though she's too young for them...Well now I understand writhe. I want to ride his hand, to move against those magical fingers until I can't fly any higher. Then he withdraws, and I almost yell at him to get back to work.

But he's staring at me, holding my gaze, which has to be dazed as cross-eyed as he's made me.

"Yes?" His deep voice rumbles against me like a purring motor, and I have no idea how his cat makes that sound. Figuring it out isn't high on my priorities list, which has exactly one thing on it: getting his fingers back to unlocking my pleasure with the slow, fast, hard, soft combination only he could know.

I don't even know what he's asking for permission to do, but I give it. "Uh huh." Because speech fails me. I'm left with only noises and moans and whimpers.

He's touching me again, pulling me to straddle him, and I want to beg him not to stop, but my words, they're gone. "You're so wet, Dot. Soaking. Is that all for me?"

Nodding, I swallow, desperately searching for my lost words, lost sense, lost ability to string together a rational thought. I close my eyes, and those golden threads bind me with delicious heat as if branding me with the mating bond. I can't give in. I won't. I...

Chase yanks me up his body to his face, and his mouth closes over me. He's biting, sucking, devouring me, and I can't breathe, can't escape the spiral that resumes faster, so much faster than before. Everything inside me coils tighter, hotter. I give in to the abandon. Dazzling silver light bursts from deep within me, shoving at the gold, twisting those threads into knots as bound as I had been.

I open my eyes and swallow a scream, my body clenching as I come hard and fast. A *whoosh* fills my head, fills the room, fills the echo of my pleasure. Heaviness settles between my shoulder blades, and Chase's eyes widen at something behind me. *No*, at some part of me.

It couldn't be.

Impossible.

Except the crash of the bedside lamp breaking, the swish of clothes being knocked aside, the rustling of something falling off the wall—those sounds tell me it's true.

I have wings. "Holy—"

# 13

## CHASE

"Holy shit." Dottie got her wings. I did that. My cougar stretches out long and lean inside me, smug and satisfied. *We* did that. Or we helped. I'm soaking up that fantasy and the reality of her gorgeous wings when she tips sideways, about to take a header into the hard floor.

Shifter reflexes save us. Snagging her wrist, I haul her back, but it's too much, too fast, and she sprawls over my chest, wings spread over us like the silkiest blanket ever. Which is worlds better than the other option, which would've been her toppled amid the shattered glass and busted pieces of stuff she's already broken with those wings unleashing.

She mumbles an apology against me.

"For what?" I ask, incredulous. "I've got you blissed-out and naked with the sexiest Fury wings spread out over me. I'd rate this as the best day ever."

"They're sexy?" She twists to glance at her drooped wings.

"The sexiest. Giant black wings—bigger than anyone's I've ever seen—cut like a butterfly with shadings of grey and silver so perfect you'd think those colors had been dipped in ink."

"Oh." Her eyes widen, and her wings flutter to their full beautiful spread. "Oh." The movement rocks her naked body against me, and I groan. If I hadn't been sporting a full hard-on before she orgasmed and outdid every other Fury in existence, I would now. The friction has me grabbing her hips to keep me from spilling like the kid I was when I first loved Dottie North.

"You're killing me." My voice sounds as though I've swallowed gravel mixed with glass. "The want of you, the taste of you." I lick my lips, catching what's left of her there. "I can't stop thinking about you, about being buried inside you, about the way you'll come around me. Mmm, will it be half as good as when you came on my tongue?"

Her wings stretch and shimmer. Oh yeah, she likes what I'm saying. Except worry flickers in her gaze.

"But Chase, what if I knock over the rest of your things? I broke your lamp and..." She peers over the side of the bed. "Whatever that was."

"It's stuff. I can buy more. Can I lick you again?"

"Yes." Her voice goes breathy, the wings dipping. "Wait, no. Look what happened last time. What if we knock the whole place down? What if my weapon to call shows up? You're unarmed."

"I'll buy a new place." I slip a finger inside her. She's so fucking wet. I can't wait to taste her again. "Plus, I'm a shifter; I *am* a weapon." She moans, and I want to lap up the sound. "But this would be your first time. It's your call. If it's too much, too fast—"

"Get naked, cat." Her twang makes *naked* sound like *nekkid,* dirty hot. The lion inside me pants for this woman. "Now."

I yank off my shirt, my breath catching when she unbuttons my jeans. The woman's not wasting time so neither do I. I strip as fast as I can, fumbling and probably looking silly since she giggles. But the second I straighten, the hunger in my Fury's eyes —the fierce need that's a razor-edge away from desperation— makes me greedy and impatient and wanting the roughness her gaze promises.

But not yet. Not until she's satisfied. Except she's wrapping her slim fingers around me, and my cat almost purrs because nothing feels as good as Dot taking charge.

"Let me," she says, and I do, nearly losing control again and again as she slides me back and forth against her folds, the slickness and heat making me insane. Then, she slips me inside her, and guilt bangs me over the head like a reminder of real life. She may be a virgin, but I'm not, and I know better.

"Shit, condom." I grab for the nightstand, almost impaling my palm on broken glass there.

She sinks lower, and I can't think. She's so tight, so wet, so fucking perfect. I don't stop her when she pulls my hand away from the glass and onto her hip.

"I'm protected. Contraception's mandatory the first five years after the turn. They don't want to risk our bodies after all we go through in the transition. From talk in town, you've been a monk the last couple of years."

"Yeah, I'm clean." I sit up, taking care not to touch her wings, and the angle has me going deeper. I'm sweating from the effort of trying to hold still while she wriggles and torments me. "Gods, Dot, you feel so good."

"I, uh..." Her shimmying stops, and she looks so damn frustrated that I want to tease her about the wrinkle between her brows, but I'm throbbing and heading toward blue balls territory here.

"What's wrong?" I fight the growl rumbling my voice. My cat does not like his woman hurting, and neither do I.

"I want you to make me yours. Not the mating stuff, but us being together—"

I take over when she doesn't finish. "Trust me, sweetheart, I'm very much interested in being together, but if you're rethinking the sex thing or the condom, just tell me." I'll stop. Don't care how much it'll kill me. Anything for my Dottie.

"It's not that." She rolls her hips, and I see stars. "I feel so full, and I'm not halfway... I mean, I might be stuck." Her words come faster, taking a moment to get past my sex-hazed fog. "I, uh, don't think I know what I'm doing, or maybe we don't fit."

I bite back a laugh. The last thing I need is a naked Fury pissed off at me for thinking I made fun of her during sex. "We fit."

"Can you take over?" She sounds heartbreakingly lost.

I almost flip her to her back, but her new wings are massive. "I don't want to hurt these." I trace the delicate edges that have the same shimmer and strength of fabric the witches call dragon scales. The texture looks tissue-thin but feels tough as poly-plas body armor. A ripple of grey and silver spreads beneath my touch.

She shudders and moans. "They're sensitive, but not like you're thinking. I ache, Chase. Make it better."

If there were more compelling words to hear from a mate, I wouldn't know, and I don't plan to find out. My sole mission in life becomes to do exactly as she's asking. My lion picks up the scent of a prowl, a hunt we were made for—satisfying our mate.

Picking her up, I walk until her wings spread against the closed door, hiking her hips higher until I take her weight, her legs locked around me. "This okay?"

"Yes." She draws the word out like a promise, a prayer, a plea.

I push inside her, stopping halfway. She's tight, a clenched fist around me. "You ready?"

"Hard and fast." Her wings quiver, quicksilver mercury undulating in a black tide.

My cat demands we give her exactly what she wants. I know gold rolls over my gaze, but she doesn't look away, doesn't ask questions, doesn't give a hint of fear. Thrusting long and deep, I savor her every sigh, her every moan, her every whimper like the finest single-malt whiskey rolling on my tongue.

Our skin slips and slaps and slides in a rhythm I race to keep. The air around us electrifies and intensifies and sizzles with something bigger than me or her. We kiss, and it's hot, hard, and demanding. My pulse hammers so loud it's all I can hear.

Our mating bond snaps, wanting her to bow to it, but my Fury doesn't, and I could never be more awestruck than by my woman. She tightens around me, digging nails into my shoulders, wrapping those glorious wings around us, and I ride out her climax until I come with her still shaking against me.

She drops her head against my shoulder, her nose going to my neck in a nuzzle my cat recognizes as a mirror of our earlier actions, another priceless gift from our mate—that of tenderness and attention.

I close my eyes and breathe past the scent of sex. Gold and silver wraps around me—bliss, pleasure, happiness. All the things I want to give her forever if she'll let me.

"Fuck, Dot. You're amazing." I open my eyes, studying her for a response, but she snuggles tighter against me, her action an answer of its own.

"Tell me we can do that again later." She sounds sleepy and satisfied.

"Whenever, however, wherever."

My lion curls up, and I'm in agreement. Wrapping Dottie in my arms, I move us to the bed, content to stay still as if we can keep this perfect moment forever. But nothing ever lasts.

A knock on my door has me thinking about ignoring it, but she stirs and props her chin atop her arm on my chest. "Probably my sisters," she says. "At least they used the front door this time."

I kiss her hair, wishing whoever was rattling my door would go away. But they don't. So I roll out of bed, throw on my jeans, and walk toward the living room with one last longing glance at my sexy, incredible mate. She hasn't accepted the mating bond, but she will with time, patience, and shifter determination. My lion's stalking her—one lick, kiss, and pet at a time.

*Bam bam bam.*

Only Furies could be so damn insistent in interrupting a big cat's nap. "Coming," I yell, buttoning my jeans. No need throwing on a shirt. I want her sisters to know she's mine, that we're destined mates.

Bring it, Furies. Whatever teasing or taunting they toss out, I can take. This blissed out and sated with my mate, absolutely nothing can bring me down.

I open the door.

Well, nothing except for a she-cougar with an enraged golden gaze. *Shit.*

# 14

## DOTTIE

I don't know who's at the door, but Chase comes back within seconds to grab his shirt.

"Stay in here," he says. "Don't come out no matter what you hear."

"What? Why—?"

He closes the door without answering. Maybe it has something to do with the killer. Or bartending or shifter business or something else Chase has going on in his life that I don't know about. Whatever it might be, with the overprotective tone he used, I'm gonna snoop for sure. I press my ear against the door— yes, the door we had mind-blowing sex against—but my wings keep getting in the way. Nothing like a telltale *swish* of body parts against wood to let everyone know I'm eavesdropping.

Grabbing my clothes, I run toward the bathroom to clean up and dress Fury fast except I can't fit through the doorway. I glimpsed my wings earlier on the bed, but they'd been down. Now, they swoop upward above my head and the tips trail down to my calves. *Great*, Chase will come back to find me naked and trapped by my own wings.

Panic curls in my gut, my heart tripping into a steady *boom*

*boom* that my shifter can probably hear from the next room. I concentrated so much these last few weeks on not being able to unfurl my wings that I didn't bother to ask how to put them away.

They look bendy, fragile even, but these babies won't budge, *thwapping* against the doorframe with the same dull "ow" that's been my constant source of bruises since I could remember. Add something to my list of knees, elbows, and hip bones to bump and bang into every doorknob, counter, or table I come across.

The third time I whack my wings into the wall, I give in, haul the sheet around me, and send a comm message to Kiva.

She answers in an instant. "What's up, baby doll? Where's the visual? Ooh, or are you getting your catnip on?"

"Do you make those cat jokes up in the moment or save them in a mental file? And would I be calling if I was...you know what?" Yes, Chase and I did *it*. No, I still won't say the word to my Fury sister. "I need your help."

"Oh, no problem. You see, the boy part goes—"

"Kiva." I whisper-shout, but it's the stern, old-school librarian kind, not a wishy-washy or weak one. "I got my wings."

"All right, why didn't you say so?"

"Maybe I should've called Sadie," I grumble. Though she would've lectured me on the safety hazards of shifter sex.

"You love me." Kiva doesn't sound the least bit concerned.

I skip straight to the point before she can kick off another tangent. "How do you get your wings to go back in?" I've watched her and Sadie tuck their wings away dozens of times in a flash, but then I'd been jealous that they could will them in or out instinctively. I hadn't focused on the mechanics. "Or keep from bumping them into stuff?"

"Let me see 'em."

No way. "How will that help?"

"Come on, show me your wings."

"I can't." A blush creeps over my skin. "I'm nearly naked."

"Well, duh, your clothes aren't slit for wings. You didn't need that until now. But I require a visual to tell me what we're working with. Are they teeny tiny wings or big honkin' massive ones? Skinny or wide? Angled or smooth? Made of blades like mine or—"

"Fine." I touch the control on my comm to allow visual. "*Now,* can you help?"

"Ooh girl, you're in the lion's bed. Way to get you some shifter lovin'. Zeus's big bolts and balls, those are some beauties on you —like butterfly wings with Fury black bleeding into silver and grey. I'll bet they're heavier than they look."

"Sooo heavy." I can already tell my upper back will be sore tomorrow.

"Run into stuff yet?"

"One or two bumps." Memories of the lamp crashing to the floor, glass shattering mid-orgasm have me wincing. I need to clean the pieces up before I leave. But first, the wings. "So how do I retract them? Is there a secret password I'm supposed to think like a spell? Or a special way to flex that tells them I don't need them anymore?"

"Huh, those would be cool options, but no. Just curl them back inside you."

"Seriously? That's all you've got? I tried to will them away. Nothing happened."

"How do you put on heels?" Kiva asks as though this is a logical progression. "You tell your feet to go in them. Same with clothes. Same with wings but in reverse. It'll get easier with practice."

I concentrate on my wings, visualize them going inside me which is super creepy. *Nada.* Nope. Not a teensy thing. "It's not working."

"Touch your nose." Kiva doesn't give me time to argue. "Just do it."

"Okay…" I put my index finger to the tip of my nose.

"Now curl your wings like rolling up two huge banners that say House of Furies Win The Derby Championships."

It's stupid. It's pointless. "It's working." My wings wrap in on themselves as though sealing away a secret.

"Now, put them away as in *poof* they're gone."

Anxiety buzzes along my nerves. "What if I can't get them back?" Or what if it takes another Chase-fueled sex session to bring them out? Not that I'm complaining, but making him follow me around as an orgasm donor doesn't seem practical.

"Stop overthinking, and don't worry so much. Trust the wings. Believe in the wings. *Be the wings.*"

"Should. Have. Called. Sadie." There's a tightening at the spot where my shoulder blades meet, a quick pins-and-needles tingling. I glance back. "Oh, hang on, they're gone."

"Awesome, now put on some clothes you brazen little hussy." Kiva makes the last sound like an endearment, a compliment of the highest order.

I end the connection and run to the bathroom, resisting the urge to test my wings to see if I can make them pop out again. Cleaning up and shimmying into my clothes, I run to press my ear to the door. Only it opens, and I stumble out.

Chase catches me.

I glance around the room. He's by himself. Whoever was here has come and gone. The small, battered dining set to our right doesn't look like a chair has been moved. No half-empty glasses sit on the well-worn coffee table. The fleece blanket tossed over the couch hasn't budged, and the only other seat in the living room has cardboard boxes stacked in it. But whatever the discussion, it's left him looking tired, weary around the eyes—less relaxed lover and more troubled soul.

"You okay?" I ask.

"You figured out your wings?" He grins at me, but tension stretches it thin, and him avoiding the question is a neon-screaming sign, but I'll play along—for now.

"You heard me talking to Kiva?"

"Shifter hearing."

"What else did you hear?"

"That you didn't ask your sisters to come get you." Sadness tinges his teasing.

I can't pretend I didn't catch the subtext. "Did something go wrong with the murder investigation? You can tell me, whatever it is. Please don't hide stuff from me. I'm a Fury; I'm not fragile."

"When I asked the wolves' marshal service for help with the investigation, there must've been a leak in their department, a spy for my dead stepfather's pride. They found me."

My stomach twists. "Did they send a representative? Was that who showed up?"

He shakes his head, mouth tight. "The alpha came herself to tell me my options." Trailing his hand along my arm in a gentle touch, he tangles his fingers with mine. "It'll be okay. She's not looking to take a life for a life, and she's reaching out to Ma to negotiate final terms."

"What does she want?" I need a real answer because the way he's sugarcoating this like a double dollop of molasses, he's softening whatever crash landing's coming.

"Cougar males are rare. Those with alpha blood even more so." His voice goes flat, as if he's narrating a documentary. "I killed a male who arguably still had some breeding potential, so she's come to claim me as a replacement, an 'upgrade' she said."

My brain stutters on *breeding*. "They want to stud you out? Like an animal?" I realize the rudeness of my comparison, but I can't take it back, and I don't want to. "They can't force you into some breeding contract. That's inhumane." Not to mention breaking my heart.

"But I'm not human, not in every state anyway. Sure, we've got shifter rights in Syn City, and the marshals are making headway, but plenty of people want us hunted down the same as dangerous animals. Shifter packs largely govern themselves, so the humans don't have to, and no one wants to risk pissing off an alpha by intervening in her decision."

"I will." I mean it. I've got wings that okay, I don't know how to use, but I'm halfway to full Fury, which has to stand for some kind of badassery.

He squeezes my hand. "While I adore that about you, I need you to stay out of this for now."

"Why? You don't think I can help?" Okay, color me ticked off and ready to argue again. If he could read my emotions through our connection, I'd be lighting every nerve as pre-Witching Wars barn red.

"No." His tone goes serious and stubborn. "You're the only one who could change her mind, which is why I'm asking you to back off for a bit."

"What do you mean?" No way am I letting him get away with that bit of cryptic. "You know a way out of this, don't you?"

"I do, but we're not pushing that escape button yet, not when I just got you back." He strokes a thumb over my knuckles as though he's afraid I'm not real or that I won't stay. I'm not sure which might be worse. "When the alpha came in, she could smell sex."

Mortification mires me down as though I've face-planted in mud with my skirt over my head. "Oh my gods, will we never have any privacy?"

"I didn't tell her who or give her any details."

"Like the fact there was a Fury in your bed with her wings stuck in the 'on' position? I'm pretty sure if you overheard my convo with Kiva, then an alpha did too. Don't they have super-powers over even what the rest of you shifters have?"

"You mean a power such as flying? I'm not the only one here with extra gifts." He says it like he's proud of me. "But no, whether or not she figured out that you're a Fury, I didn't mention you in connection to the unfinished mating bond she sensed."

"Oh no." I need to sit. Fumbling behind me for the couch, I let him help me off my feet before my wobbling knees give out. How far I've fallen from soaring close to flying only a few minutes ago. "Others can tell that's a thing between us? That you and I—"

"Only shifters can sense the potential. It's to keep us from messing with someone else's mate. And maybe immortals can feel the bonds, too, since the Fury who turned you appeared to me. Other than that, whatever our bond might be now or might become later, that's just between you and me." He's all determination and passion now, selling his truth like it's the only one in the world, and I'm all for cashing out and buying in except for one thing.

"But you said I could change her mind? The alpha's? How?"

Emotions flicker across his face too fast for me to read. "Peaches thinks—"

"Peaches? A cougar pride follows an alpha named Peaches?"

"Yeah, well, blood and fighting ability outweigh everything else in shifter hierarchy, and I'm betting she got a lot of practice scrapping in the schoolyard with that name. Anyway, she believes the woman destined to be my mate has rejected me."

"Me? I rejected you?"

"I didn't say that, and I sure as hell didn't give her information about you or what's been going on in Syn City since she might use any details against me. Peaches has given me a few weeks to either make amends with my mate...you...or to settle my job and life here before I go with her."

"How could you even think of leaving here with some random alpha pussy named Peaches? You're gambling with your future, with *our* future—"

He pulls me closer. "I took away nine years of us possibly being together, our chance to be a couple during your first life, because I didn't tell you where I'd gone or what had happened in my family. I took away your choice, and my mistake stole whatever chance we had of being happy *then*. I'm not letting Peaches or me or anyone else take away your choice this time."

He snarls with the last, his lion peeking out from behind green eyes.

"What are you talking about? If doing whatever I need to do to accept this bond means you—"

He doesn't let me finish. "It'd mean forever, Dot, binding yourself to me forever. Now, you made it clear before sex that you weren't ready for the mating bond, and I agree. In the last month or so, you've been murdered in a place guaranteed to be safe, you've been brought back as a Fury, you've had to deal with a shitload of change, you saw Neda be displayed like some sicko's kill trophy at The Rink, and now your teenaged, human cousin has come to visit. The last thing you need to add to your load right now is figuring out whether or not you want to spend forever with a man you haven't completely forgiven for running out on you years ago."

"I..." I want to argue with him, to tell him he's wrong, but I can't, and from the look in his eyes, he knows it.

"Give yourself time," he says. "Give me the weeks I've been offered before the alpha's decision comes due. Give *us* those weeks. My mother's my alpha. She'll be allowed a say and can probably buy me time until I track down the killer since that's a blood vow. We have a few days, so take 'em before you make a decision you might regret. Life with a shifter's not easy, and your second life's already hard enough." He traces his hand over my hair. "Nothing needs to change unless or until you decide differently, and I don't want to wonder in ten years if you picked me because you felt you had to. A forced mating isn't a real one, and you deserve better."

The raw honesty of what he said hits me like a triple-blocker blow on the rink, sending me skidding with nothing to hold on to except for him.

Until we catch a killer.

Until I decide forever.

Or until they take him away.

## 15

---

## CHASE

Insisting that Dottie take the time she needs to decide about our future and the mating bond is the right thing to do—and the hardest. We spend our days apart but our nights together.

Tonight, a week away from the serial killer's next deadline, my Dottie's flying. Using her wings got off to a rough start in the beginning, but she's able now to kick off, fly a fairly straight path, and land without completely crashing. Kiva and Sadie flank her, helping her navigate the normal Fury flight path. Maizie makes for a more encouraging teacher, offering tips whenever she and the WannaBe twins dash by. The night sky fills with black wings shimmering silver in the moonbeams that sneak between the heavy tangle of treetops.

Connie sits beside me on a fallen log, and she's both her cousin's biggest cheerleader and critic. Long brown hair pulled into twin knots on top of her head, big brown eyes, freckles across her nose, and a dimpled grin that she uses to score anything and everything she wants, she's almost a mini-me of Dottie, and I can't help but think of the girl I fell for in Petunia who is now banking her wings to zip around obstacles fifty feet off the ground.

"Ooh, cuz, hang a hard right," Connie yells, peeking from between her fingers toward Dot's latest attempt to dodge the trees around the Fury house. After deafening me for the tenth time in as many minutes, she lowers her voice and elbows me. "She's gonna take out half the cypress trees. They need to chop those vines and moss down to the roots. They're a flight hazard. Might as well be a spider's web with the way Dottie gets caught in them."

I grin at the teenager who thinks she's a flying expert now. "The moss and heavy vine growth serve a purpose. The Furies keep them as camouflage, a defense to protect their home." To go along with their poison garden that I suspect Sadie might've planted given the huge amount of wolf's bane blooming. Then, there's the high-power weaponry they have mounted on the roof that I can only sniff out with shifter senses.

"Pfft. Not like anyone would be stupid enough to take on the Furies." Connie tugs her pink-and-purple-polka-dotted wrist comm from under the sleeve of her official derby shirt—black, of course, with winged avengers powering down the rink to support her cousin's House. "I still say they need a gardener. You know I've taken on Dottie's cleaning gigs, or the one's they'll let a minor do anyway. Those are shit jobs. I don't know how she's managed to keep up with them all for so long."

I've talked with Dot about her old job, and some of the toxic clean-ups she fronted make me sick to think about, her sweating in her hazmat suit as she takes care of the extreme literal dirty work. "She took the high-risk jobs because they paid better."

"Because her mom has gotta be kept in pills and booze."

"And because Dot put food on the table and made sure the power stayed on."

"True." Connie heaves an epic sigh that could've been heard by every shifter in the city. "She made sure I didn't go hungry either. My dad sort of forgets about me when he's on long hauls.

Sometimes he leaves cash to cover groceries. Sometimes he doesn't."

I knew the cousins were tight. With Dot's dad taking off before she knew him and Connie's mom dying of a radiation-spawned illness that was a Witching Wars leftover, they didn't have anyone else. "Dottie loves you."

"Then why won't she let me stay here?"

Ah, I should've realized the kid who's too smart for anyone's good set up this trap for me to plod my big lion paws into. "You know Dot's got her reasons for wanting you out of Syn City."

"The serial killer. Yeah, I showed up on the crime scene, so I know the danger. Let's face it. Petunia has its own risks."

I stare at her. "You mean someone might blow past the one four-way stop sign?"

"No, that's ancient history. Somebody ran over that sign a couple of years ago, and the town's two cops decided not to replace it. I'm talking that I'll never have a future if I stay stuck in that tiny town. I might as well sign up for permanent bake sale duty with the blue-haired ladies in the Coalition Against Magic Operators."

"You know we're from a redneck town when the biggest organization goes by the acronym CAMO."

"Riiight?"

"But it's your redneck town, and it's a good place, a *safe* place."

"You don't know that. There's danger everywhere. We're one trigger-happy human or rogue shifter away from a mass murder. No offense."

I know how most humans view shifters—we're wild animals who need to be tagged and bagged. "Still, that's a potential danger. The serial killer here is an actual one. Dottie's right to be scared for you, for her, for all of us."

"But I've been talking to the Furies, and I could really make a future here. I fit in. Coach loves me. She says I could help around The Rink, sell concession or merchandise for a part-time job. Or maybe help that creep Marty keep up with the props. I don't like how he looks at my cousin."

The kid has amazing instincts. Even with Marty being crossed off the list of suspects, I still can't stand the way he stares at Dottie like a missed opportunity, as though she could've been his girl if she hadn't become a Fury, found me, or whatever other reasons he's set up in his mind as the only obstacles. "Yeah, he's weird. But let's say we caught the serial killer and your cousin and the others went full Fury on him. Even still, having a job wouldn't be your only issue if you moved here. Your dad would miss you."

"My dad wouldn't notice I'm gone, no more than Dottie's mom misses her. Guess it runs in the family. But here? I would have Dottie, and I would try to help her out in her new life as much as she has always been there for me. I could help you with the investigation stuff since it's been taking up every hour you aren't with us or working at the bar."

"I don't think telling Dottie that you want to help me track down a murderer will be a point in your favor on the safety argument. Call it a hunch."

"But some of the women at The Rink? They told me the school here has an excellent record, that other parents beg the Syndicate to let their kids come, but they only allow the families of House members. Plus, they would let me do college-level courses. Do you know who all makes up the Syndicate?"

By now, I've grown used to the whip-fast change of subjects that comes with Connie's conversations. "No one except the Syndicate knows who the actual members are. We peasants don't need to know."

She acts as if I didn't speak. "I wonder if they allow student workers. Maybe I could figure out a way to stay on even after I graduate if I'm working for the Syndicate. Can you put in a good word for me to stay with my cousin? Pleeease?"

"Oh no, I'm not getting involved. This decision will be up to the two of you."

"Don't drag him into this, Connie." Dottie skids to a jerky landing in front of us, her wings flapping as though she's reaching to catch herself too late. Her boots leave slide marks in the mud. "I told you it's not safe. Maybe after we figure out the murders and things get back to normal."

"Like anything will ever be normal here." Connie points at Dot's giant wings that've gone solid black. "And I could help Chase with the investigation. I'm good at organizing stuff."

I raise my palms and keep my mouth shut, not that either of the two gives me time to interrupt.

"I *died*." Dottie yanks her wings in as if she's been doing it forever, the leaves rustling behind her and her tank top rippling. "So you'll have to forgive me if I seem unreasonable in keeping you safe, but I'm not gambling with the chance that the same could happen to you. And don't even bring up the Fury thing. I have no idea how the immortals pick, who they choose, or if my second life will end up being something we will all regret."

"Ugh." Connie practically snarls in a damn good cougar impersonation. "You don't realize how cool you've always been, how friggin' legendary you are now."

"My skull getting cracked open like a walnut? Not something to envy. You're not coming to live here."

"Don't you want me with you?" The teen's voice turns into a wail. My shifter senses say waterworks and a full toddler-worthy tantrum are incoming.

Dottie's shoulders droop. "You know that's not—"

"You don't love me." Connie jumps up and sprints away toward the swamp.

Do I chase after her? Or comfort Dottie who looks like the kid slapped her?

Kiva dive-bombs from the sky, dipping to float above us. "Hormones at fifteen—a bitch for all of us, am I right? I'll get her." And she's gone, kicking up leaves and splashing mud.

"Connie didn't mean that last bit." Sure, I'm stating the obvious, but the lost-my-kitten look on Dottie's face has me rushing to reassure her. "Kiva will talk her down."

"I can't let her stay, not with a serial killer targeting women. I have to get her out of Syn City. We'll pack tonight, and she can head out tomorrow. That way, she's gone a few days before the sixth."

Before he collects his next victim. She doesn't say it, and neither do I.

She sits next to me. "How's the investigation coming?"

"I've waded through hours of surveillance captures and dug through thousands of travel records, ticket sales, merch receipts, and hotel registrations. So far, I've got no common threads for travelers on the sixth of the last few months. I'm not a detective, but my gut tells me we're dealing with someone who lives here, and the facts support my conclusion."

"Reasonable assumption. Someone who knows us well, who could access the locker room, who got close enough to Neda to murder her." She pushes out the last as if she's forcing the words.

"I'm waiting on clearance to access employment hire records, personnel files, and discipline write-ups. I didn't even know the Houses kept stuff on us grunts who work at The Rink and in the pleasure district. Guess it makes sense since most of us stick around. Finding work for supernaturals in the human world has gotten harder. Plus, I met a cute, kickass Fury who's bound here by magic and fate."

She bumps against me. "Coach could help you get the records on the workers. Maybe on House members, too."

"You get along well with her, don't you?"

"I got lucky as far as Houses go. I've never had someone in a boss position who truly cares about me. She's more mom most days than an actual coach. I can't imagine trying to keep a houseful of Furies in line. It must be a sorority on steroids plus supernatural powers times a bijillion. She reminds me of when I used to hang out at your house and your Ma would come check on us, give us cookies, remind us to do our homework. Plus, she adores Connie. Lets my cousin follow her around like a trainee."

"I'm glad you've got Coach, and I'll ask her about the House records. Can you imagine if this connects with one of the Houses? The Syndicate would go berserk. No way do I think any of the seven Houses might actually be home to a killer." When she gives me extreme side-eye and then glances at her fellow Furies, I amend what I said. "Well, not one killed outside of your deity daughter duties."

Kiva brings Connie back into the flight pattern, tossing her from one winged crazy to another and the teenager laughs as though it's a ride at the county fair.

"Furies?" Coach's voice booms from the porch above, and everyone freezes. "Don't drop her." With the annoyed statement, she goes back inside.

Above, I can hear teasing from the Furies flying back and forth so fast that I can't be sure who's saying what. *Ooh, Coach's pet. Don't drop the little human. As if we'd be so klutzy; that's Dottie's job. Coach's favorite can't fly but she can bounce. Heads up, catch the kid.*

Connie laughs the entire time, and Dottie's muscles lose some of the cranked-to-the-max tension she's been carrying every time I see her unless I can get her to forget her problems long enough to climax. Which hasn't been an issue. My Fury might be stressed, but she brings that same ferocity to the bedroom, and my cat loves the way she goes from all work to complete play in an instant. My woman's sexy and strong and scared for her baby cousin. I can't blame her.

"Don't doubt your instincts about taking care of Connie. She thinks she's grown, and she almost is. But not yet. You can treat her like a cub for as long as you want with the way you two were brought up together."

"Thanks. I think sending her home for now at least is the

right call but remind me of that later tonight when she's screaming about me packing her stuff."

"I'll be working at The Rink, stocking the bar and cleaning before the next bout since we sold out of practically everything with the droves of drunks here for the Muse's concert. But feel free to message me. I'm already missing our time together tonight."

She leans into me, snuggling her cheek against my shoulder like we'd been made to fit each other. "I hate to ask, but how are things with Peaches?" She says the name in a disgusted tone like she might say *putrid*.

I don't walk to talk about it. "She's a true alpha cougar. I'm not sure what went down between her and Ma, but Peaches hasn't bugged me since she came by the other day to say bids on me have been pouring in from the local cougars looking for a temporary mate."

"She's auctioning you off? Why? How?"

I shrug. "Most shifter packs wouldn't, but mountain lion prides have their own rules. We're better than the wolves. Not as crazy as the bears."

"I could say we're mates—"

"Don't." I can't stand a pity offer. Or that she'd half-ass something as life changing as mates. "We still have time."

She nods, not looking like she believes me. But we have a few days. I pull her into my lap, rubbing my nose against hers in a sweet substitute for a kiss that has the Furies making fun of us, but my cat loves the gesture, and my girl melts against me like caramel candies in the summer heat. We stay like that until I have to leave for work.

"I'll come by and see you and Connie tomorrow before she leaves." In between digging through one box of records and another, hoping each receipt or handwritten scrawl leads me to the killer.

"I'll miss you tonight, but I'll make it up to you." She nips at my mouth, the playfulness delighting my cat and the sexiness making me want to kiss her until her wings come out. But there's no time before my shift starts.

"Promise?" My voice becomes an almost purr with my lion so close to the surface.

"Uh huh." She speaks so softly that I wouldn't catch her words but for my shifter hearing. "I've been wanting to try me on top with my wings out and maybe a little flying if you're up for it."

"Oh, I'll be up for it. My cat can climb however high you need me."

She smacks at my thigh with a grin, and I want to catch hold of this moment, this easiness between us and save the memory if things don't go the way I hope, if my Fury can't commit her second life to shifter world standards, if she's the one leaving me this time around, or if I'm the only one who believes we're truly fated mates.

I carry the happiness of her laugh against my lips, the taste of her delight, the sound of her satisfied sigh, and the heat of her touch against the chill of The Rink's blasting AC and the thumping tech-electro-dance mix that I don't know who chose, but I wish they'd switch it off. I'm back and forth between the loading dock and the stock room for hours, checking the shipments and carting boxes of booze. Plus, I help the deer shifter who's been stuck cataloging a truckload of new merch. She's more of an accountant with a bad back and bum knee than an athlete, and stacking the heavy product doesn't bother me.

I like being at the bar, flirting with patrons, serving up drinks, riding their excited buzz, and snooping on the gossip flowing as freely as alcohol. But the stock room's secluded and usually quiet, although tonight, the grating *bump-bump* of the music's driving beat gives me a headache.

It's late by the time I wrap up, and the deer shifter left a while ago, heading home to her kids. Sometimes, the cleaning crew is here depending on when the shipments arrive, but tonight, there's no chlorine and pine smell. Guess it means I'm the only one left, other than whoever's cranked the lousy music.

After locking the stock room and securing the bar, I flip the keys into my pocket and head for the staff door off the side of the mezzanine. A few steps into the circular walkway that makes up the outer loop of The Rink, I catch a familiar scent, one that's not quite human, the one I found in the locker room, one I could almost detect at Dottie's murder scene beneath the sensory overload that was the immortal Fury.

Inhaling, I sort through the odors and backtrack until I find that smell again. I can't place the origin—sort of human, but not entirely, it's neither shifter nor House member. Sniffing my way toward the audience seats, I pick up the slight stench and track its trail. Curling back and forth, the scent trace travels down to the track, hitting me stronger on the northern curve. I crouch and run my hands over the concrete that's usually smooth as glass for the derby skaters. Here, bumps and grooves catch on my fingertips, as if someone tore their claws through the concrete. Or poured a salted varnish across the top and nicked the finish.

Other smells flood my senses here—sweat, leather, and derby stank beneath the pyro smoke. Coach's perfume comes through stronger than the other Furies as though it's recent. Nearby, I pick up Dottie's roses but mixed with vanilla cupcake, Connie's scent. Closer to the trap doors in the pit floor, the not-quite-human trail begins again, and with it mingles those of Connie and Coach.

My heart speeds up, my breathing shrinks to shallow, and my lion's senses narrow to stalking that trail, hoping to hell I only find my imagination chasing its tail at the end of the path. I stop at the locker room. The same scents are here but weak.

A stronger lead heads toward the janitor's supply stacks. Yeah, The Rink's big enough that a simple closet won't suffice. The cleaning crews require rows of sanitizers, polishes, detergents, and disinfectants. Those shelves sandwich between the sprawling maintenance section and the props department in the behind-the-scenes operations needed to keep The Rink running.

I pound on the metal door. "Hello?" Last thing I need is to sneak up on my woman's Coach and her colossal battle ax, but the deafening roar of fans inside overpowers anyone's answer. I push into the room, something heavy catching on the door, and the place reeks. The scent I followed is here, yeah, but drenched in bleach and blood. My stomach rolls, my breathing cuts to choppy, and my throat tightens like a wrench cranks around my neck.

A rack has toppled against the door, spilling chemicals across the floor. Fumbling around the fallen shelves for the light switch, I slap at the plastic and unsheathe my claws and flash my fangs. There's been a fight. Boxes and bottles have been knocked to the ground. A can of powered cleaner has rolled, spraying a white arc. I hurry toward the strongest smell of blood, stopping when I find a red handprint on a box—delicate fingers, slight palm, a woman's hand. Streaks of the same show where she clung to or clawed the wall going toward the props department.

The noisy fans drown out anything else. Someone could be hiding, waiting to ambush me. My lion bristles at the possibility of being prey instead of predator, but I keep going. Blood spatter drips across the floor and walls. A sledgehammer lays on the tile as if dropped in a rush, the handle caught on an overturned trash can. Not two feet away, silver hair streaked with blood covers the face of a woman wearing black splayed out over the ground.

"Coach?" I rush to her side, dropping beside her and pushing back her hair. But she's gone. Her eyes stare fixed at a far-off point, the whites around the dark more visible than I've ever seen them. Half of her skull has been cracked open. She has met her second death.

I freeze, unsure of what to do next. Message the House of Furies? Try to track the killer's scent further? But then I'd have to leave her here, and abandoning Coach's body seems so wrong. I glance around, catching sight of a wrist comm on the ground. Pink with purple polka dots. *Connie.*

He's taken Connie.

Panic overtakes rational thought. Risking any punishment the Syndicate might hand down, I shift to mountain lion form so I can run my fastest. I sprint toward the House of Furies, sliding to a stop at the base and screaming until Furies drop from the sky to surround me. Most have their weapons to call in their hands, landing in warrior poses as if ready to do battle.

Dottie lands in front of me, her wings shaking as though nervous energy sparks through them. "Chase?"

I shift, not giving a damn about my nudity. "He killed Coach, and he has Connie."

# 16

## DOTTIE

I can't breathe. My world whirls and goes fuzzy at the edges. Thoughts and emotions bombard me like hornets from a nest I've kicked, and those feelings fly away so fast, so far that I can't catch a single one.

Coach was beaten and bludgeoned the same way I died.

Connie's gone.

She's gone, and I don't know how to find her. We've struck out for almost two months on tracking the killer, Neda died for our failures, and now my baby cousin is out there alone in a city she doesn't know with strangers and a serial killer when she shouldn't have come here in the first place, wouldn't have if it hadn't been for me.

I've done this.

I've put her at risk.

I've gotten her kidnapped and my mentor killed.

Chase stands in front of me, and I've no idea how long he's been there. More than a couple of seconds with the way he stares at me as though I might break. I blink and glance around. Everyone left, and I missed the how and why.

"They've gone to bring Coach's body home," he says.

"He killed her." Such simple, weighty words.

"He did."

"The same way he murdered me."

"Yeah. Since it's her second death, the Furies will follow the old ways so her soul can find peace."

"She shouldn't have died."

"No, sweetheart. She shouldn't have died either time."

Hearing my words repeated back to me makes this horror real. "The immortal Fury brought me back to avenge my killer, to stop the murders. I failed her. Look what's happened. If Coach couldn't defend herself, how am I supposed to confront him? How am I supposed to save Connie?" My voice rises in pitch, worries tumbling out faster and faster. "I can barely fly a straight line, and I don't have my weapon to call. I'm not even a full Fury yet. I can't help her. If she dies, it'll be my fault, and—"

"Shh." Chase pulls me into a hug—a naked hug. I'd forgotten about him shifting. He's warm and safe and so strong, but what if being close to me gets him killed?

"I can't do this."

"Do what, sweetheart?"

"Any of this. I came here on a hunch, for what? To have an adventure, to get out of Petunia? Well, it worked. But now I've made a mess of everything. I died and now I'm stuck in Syn City for a life I never expected or wanted. Coach and Neda have been murdered. Connie's probably going to die because I led her here and didn't force her to leave sooner. You're about to be auctioned off as a stud cougar. I'll be stuck in a second life knowing I've destroyed everyone I cared about." I tense and my wings open with a whoosh, ready to take to the sky and run away.

"Don't run, Dot. If you run, my cat will chase. I won't be able to stop the instinct." He relaxes his hold, but his posture holds both a plea and a predator's promise. "We will find Connie. She's a fighter. The smudged handprints, stuff knocked over? She struggled. He didn't take her easily."

"What if he punishes her, tortures her for putting up a fight? He's accustomed to sneak attacks from behind."

"A coward. He won't know what to do with her. Coach's death might've given Connie seconds she needed. What if he'd meant to kill them both, and she changed the plans somehow? She's smart, and she's tough. Hell, she's a Petunia girl. He'll have to think fast to stay ahead of her."

"But his deadline, the sixth of the month, comes in less than a week."

"That gives her time to survive and time for us to find her. We can do this together, but you've gotta believe in her and in yourself. You're not alone anymore. You've got me and your sisters. Even in their shock and grief, Sadie and Kiva didn't want to leave you."

"They didn't?"

"No, they wouldn't go until I promised to stay here with you until they returned. The Furies will call in the other Houses."

"The other Houses didn't do anything before when Coach asked them to step up security."

"Coach's murder and Connie's kidnapping will change their minds. Your death didn't count to them because the immortals turned you—a fated destiny they could say. But this? Neda proves the killer has gotten bold with his displays. They can't risk a human, especially not a human child, becoming a public relations disaster. The Syndicate runs this city on the money the tourists bring. Maybe their greed will save your cousin."

My gut rolls and writhes, a roiling, stabbing pain as though it's morphed into a den of the water moccasins that slither along with the sea hags. "I can't count on them wanting money badly enough to do the right thing when that means Connie's life."

"We won't. We'll find her. Whether the Houses help or not, we'll rescue her."

"How?"

"I know her scent, but it'd help if you have some of her

clothes, unwashed if possible. I can ask the other shifters to scout. There have been no ferries in or out today, so she's still here."

Panic sizzles over my skin, and my wings shake violently. "What if he found another way across the swamp?"

Chase shakes his head. "Everything we know points to the killer being a local—him being here on the sixth of every month, the access he has, the way he knows The Rink. He's got to work there."

Suspicion pricks at me, a nagging sensation that stings the spot where my wings meet my back, where a proverbial knife might be if he's right and we both know the murderer. "How long have you been in Syn City?"

"Three, almost four years."

"You're sure the killer's a him?"

"Yeah, judging by the scent."

"Yet you don't recognize him by scent alone? How's that possible? You would've run into him, especially if he works at The Rink."

"I don't know. We went door to door through the staff quarters, and the Houses don't allow males to live anywhere but there. Maybe he's masking it? Cloaking potions cost a lot and can be unreliable, but they exist."

I haven't heard of them, but the past month has proven I didn't know much about supernaturals other than how to clean up after them. "I'd hoped to have Connie booked for the first ferry out tomorrow. Her clothes are packed upstairs, including the ones she wore earlier today. We should have something to almost fit you in the House wardrobe as well."

In the bedroom where Connie stayed, I can't move without seeing her in the room. Acting on autopilot, I unzip the suitcase I'd packed for her and wait while Chase goes through each piece checking for the strongest scents. Sitting on the bed my cousin slept in, I hold the derby jersey she was so proud of. "I shouldn't have let her go to the track—not even with Coach." Gods, how have I lost both of them in the same day?

"Why were they there? No one had practice or meetings scheduled. Other than me and a female deer shifter putting away a shipment delivered yesterday, The Rink was deserted."

"A report of a tampering with the track came in. I told Connie not to go, not to pester Coach no matter that the woman didn't mind her inviting herself to tag along. She has a—" I stop, force myself to rephrase in the past tense. "Had a soft spot for my cousin." I still can't imagine an unstoppable force like Coach being gone.

"I noticed the problem with the track. Coach would've wanted to investigate before letting any of you skate at tomorrow's practice."

I nod, not able to talk about how the woman worried over her Furies as though the House was a grown-up reform school filled with sensitive personalities instead of a fighting force of deity daughters. She'd shown me a stern version of kindness, and I'd wanted to impress her instead of being the late bloomer who struggled to get her wings, her weapon to call, or her cousin out of Syn City.

Chase sits beside me, the mattress creaking with his weight. I lean into him, breathing in his masculine scent beneath the powdery fresh detergent and fruity body spray of his borrowed threads.

"What can I do?" I ask him.

"You're not going to like the answer." His rumbling voice reassures me no matter what he's saying. At least he has an answer. I'm floundering like a fish caught on an invisible line.

"Today's been horrible. I don't know that any advice will make it worse."

"The best thing you can do is wait."

My heart sinks to my stomach before *ba-bumping* its way to my feet. "You're right. I hate that."

He squeezes my hand. "With a terrible, brutal death like this, emotions run high. Blame gets passed around like an explosive potion that no one wants to handle. Between your recent turn and Connie's kidnapping, you'll be the most convenient target for some of the Houses. It'd be easier for whoever steps into Coach's role to negotiate assistance if you're not visible. Or they'll blame you for me missing something in the search, arguing you distracted me." He sounds as though he might welcome a fight but not this one. "Plus, without your weapon to call, Sadie and Kiva will be worried about keeping you safe while you're away from the House of Furies rather than focusing on Connie."

The man makes sense, and his firm but gentle hold on me softens the raw honesty so I can find the logic in his words instead of seeing only the hurt. "All right." I steady myself by concentrating on the patterns in the hardwood beneath my feet, the flecked paint on one wall that looks like a blade had caught there, the softness of Connie's shirt in my hand. "I can wait for now." I can't promise any more.

Chase holds me, our silence a heavy blanket around me acting as both a strain and a shield. I can't dwell on any of our problems, not together or apart, because Connie comes first. We sit there a few more moments, the agonizing tangle of emotions not mattering so much as the comfort we take from each other.

Sadie taps on the partially open door, the soft knock hesitant. She stares at Chase. "Maizie's been tapped as Coach's replacement, and she needs to talk to you about the search. I'll stay with her."

Great, she's talking about me as if I'm not here. I must look shell-shocked like those Witching Wars fallout refugees in the hologram archives. "I'm okay," I lie.

"Sure." Her tone says she doesn't believe me, but she waits for Chase to kiss me goodbye and leave the room before calling me out on the fib. "How are you really?"

I open my mouth to lie again, but a choked sob comes out instead. "Sad. Scared."

"Yeah." She sits beside me, taking the spot Chase just left. "It's been a fucked-up day. We'll get your cousin back."

"But not Coach."

"No." She rubs her chest as if her heart hurts the way mine does. "Not Coach. I thought she didn't like me much, but she only made me work harder. She did what she could to bring out the best of a bunch of murdered and turned women who came to her carrying dumpster-planet-sized trauma."

"What will we do without her?"

"Maizie stepped up. She's shaken but solid. Actually, I came to talk to you about what happens next."

The way she said those last words? Not good, not good at all. "Are they kicking me out of the Furies?"

"No. Once a Fury, you're stuck with us."

"Until second death comes." Like it had for Coach.

"Yeah, so do us a favor and stay alive this time. Kiva and I wouldn't fit with a different third. You're meant to be our sister."

"I need to look for Connie."

"You can't. That's why I'm here. The Houses are planning a full-scale raid of the staff quarters, the hotels, anywhere someone could be hiding. We'll find your cousin."

"Oh, but that's wonderful. Chase took some of her clothes so shifters can help track the scent. I can start—"

"No." Sadie puts her hand on my arm. "You can't come with us for the search, at least not yet."

"Maizie said that?"

"Leaving you out wasn't her idea, but she needs the support of the other Houses. Some refused to help at all if you went with us. Besides, even if you found the killer, you don't have your weapon to call. You can't go full Fury yet."

"I don't understand. She's *my* cousin. I'm broken-hearted about Coach, but I'm terrified for Connie—"

Sadie cuts me off again. "The Fury way isn't sadness or fear. It's vengeance, bloodthirsty vengeance. Can you kill without hesitation?"

"I think so." Maybe. Probably.

She shakes her head. "You have to remain inside the House of Furies until Maizie says otherwise. The Huntresses and their leader? They're ready to ground us all. You need to stay so the rest of us can be out there looking for her."

"You don't understand. She's the only family I have who loves me exactly as I am." My voice breaks, and I slam my mouth shut as if I can swallow the pain.

"I had a family." Sadie's voice goes flat, eerily distant, which sounds worse than when she's sarcastic and throwing verbal shade. "I'll do everything I can to find yours, even work with your cat."

At her most serious, she still can't stand him, and I'm done with her open dislike of my...my...whatever he might be. "Why do you hate Chase?" I snap out the question with the cutting bite of her whip.

"It's not him. He's tolerable—a reliable bartender, keeps to himself, decent guy other than his vanity and his arrogance, although maybe those come with being a cat. I suppose you could do worse. He could be a wolf." She spouts hatred as easily as most people discuss the weather.

"So you're simply a bigot against all shifters for something they can't change?"

She gives me an arctic glare. "You don't know how I died, do you?"

The memory of her talking at The Rink about her past as a kitchen witch, about her family, haunts me. "They condemned you as a witch? So you think because they murdered you out of hate that it's okay for you to do the same?"

"I wasn't outed for witchcraft. I died because my sister loved the wrong man."

What? I'm missing something here, something huge. "I don't understand. Her guy killed you?"

"My older sister dated a wolf shifter for years. We all loved him." She sounds so bitter, so heartbroken. "The police said he must've gone rogue. I heard my sister's screams. I tried to cast a protection spell, but I couldn't pull the pieces together fast enough. He slaughtered her, me, my parents, my baby sister. I don't remember being torn to pieces. The cops say that's a blessing." She swallows hard and presses her lips into a tight, trembling line. "I blacked out and woke up to my second life in Syn City as a Fury. I don't talk about it much, so do me a favor as my new sister, and don't repeat it. Not even to your mate."

"He's not my—"

"He is. Everyone knows that but you." She blows out a shaky breath. "Dottie, I should be the last person to tell you to stop messing around and make that shifter—man, mountain lion, or whatever—your mate, but the truth's obvious if you'd stop running from this life and decide what you want. Or maybe figure out who you are *now*. You're not some broke girl from Nowheresville. You're a badass Fury with a cat who loves you more than himself, which seems to be a rare thing. So consider using this time on lockdown to do something about it. Now, come on. Your restriction shouldn't keep you off the flight deck. You can say goodbye to him. With any luck, we'll be back in the hour with your cousin safe and one of us carrying your killer's head."

I hold tight to her first hope and squash the visual that her second provokes to keep my tummy from turning. Saving Connie is all that matters now.

Outside, the night wraps around me, its shadows comforting. Maizie leads the House in what looks like battle preparations instead of a search, radiating devastated loss as much as leadership. Furies gather in their triads, checking gear and gathering weapons.

A few knives, small axes, and a handgun have been tossed to

the side. Furies typically don't carry guns. Something about the old gods promising a vicious curse upon anyone who wields guns against an immortal's child—a curse that would wipe out the offender's entire family. The memory of Coach teaching me the consequences of weapons, the differences in them, the ways to wield them, the possibilities for mine to call slams into me, and I put my hand out to steady myself, meeting solid muscle.

"Here to knock me off the porch again?" Chase teases, only I can't laugh, don't know if I'll be able to again any time soon.

I can't shake the sudden dread that pulses through me. "Come back safely to me."

He strokes my cheek. "I'm a cat. I always land on my feet."

With his sort of promise, over the side he goes, claws out and making fast time toward the ground. Kiva and Sadie meet my gaze, nodding as if swearing silent vows, then take to the sky.

Left alone in a big house with nothing but my fear and worry, I gather the weapons left behind and head into the training room. I'll change into my battle gear that's never seen a real fight and work until I find my weapon to call or they find Connie.

They'll be back soon.

They promised.

And promises are all I have right now.

## 17

# CHASE

THE STAFF QUARTERS GENERALLY SMELL OF FOOD, FAMILY, AND familiar comforts. It's one of many reasons I like living here. Tonight, the massive housing complex reeks of fear, rage, and grief. Understandable with the large population of retired House members. A murdered Coach—especially from the Furies— means anyone could be a future victim.

A Gorgon skater who spends most of her time at The Rink in the penalty box bars the front entrance. Marauder, they call her on the track, and I can't remember her real name. She points at me. "The cat can't come in. For Hephaestus's sake, he's a bartender. What kind of skills could he add to a search when the Mad Maes already have the party covered?"

"He's with us," Maizie says.

The Gorgon sneers, and I want to claw her face off. The Furies have enough to deal with in the aftermath of losing Coach.

"Got something to hide?" I ask, not able to resist batting at her, pushing her to a fight if that's what she really wants—whatever it takes to get past her and look for Connie. Although, judging by the noise level coming from inside, the sheer number of people will have destroyed any scent trail. "Don't worry about me accusing you. I can't scent anything on you past the stink of jealousy."

"You friggin' furball." The Gorgon gets in my face, and I don't budge. "Your Fury started all this. If she'd have stayed dead, the killer wouldn't have come after our Houses."

Her talking about Dottie has me flashing fangs. Maybe I'll go through her instead of around her.

"Whoa." Kiva pushes to the front, wings tucked close but flashing silver blades. "You talking about my sister, Moron the Gorgon?"

"Don't call me that." The Gorgon keeps up the tough tone, but her angry gaze loses some of its confidence. Her scent changes, going more afraid than arrogant. She may stand a head higher and carry more weight on her bigger frame, yet there's no mistaking the fear the smaller Fury invokes. "You know my name's Mauran."

"But is it? Because the other fits you, and it rhymes." Kiva sounds so gleeful that it's scary. "Don't make us kick your ass off the track as much as we do on it."

"You don't—"

"Move." Stepping forward, Sadie cuts the Gorgon off. "Tonight's not the night to mess with the Furies. We'll cut you down on our way to vengeance."

I'm ninety percent certain a fight's coming, and I wouldn't bet against a House that lost a beloved mother figure only hours ago. There's mean, and then there's motivated. Plus, the Gorgons have strength, but not the Furies' speed.

Maizie intervenes. "Consult your House if you need to, Gorgon, but we Furies have the right of way. Vengeance is our duty, and this one's personal. He killed our Coach and Dottie."

"He murdered a Nymph, too," Mauran adds.

"See, there's the whole moron thing," Kiva says. "What do you think the Nymphs will do? Slay him with sex appeal? Screw him to death?"

Holding up a hand, Maizie does the supreme leader thing again, commanding quiet with a simple gesture. "I'm head of the House of Furies, and I tell you to let us pass with the shifter unless you challenge my leadership on behalf of your House."

The Gorgon looks surprised for a split-second, her eyes widening, and then moves. "No, Coach."

Maizie's stern expression shifts to sadness for a moment, the new title seeming to press down on her shoulders like a physical weight. I feel sorry for her, sorry for all the Furies. She should've had years more to prepare, should've had a peaceful transition. Instead, she's arguing politics and searching for a murderer of deity daughters. "Furies," she calls, and every warrior with wings locks gazes on her. "We search each home, each room, each closet —no matter who else has searched it before. Let no one leave until we finish. Got it?"

"Yes, Coach." The solemn promise comes from all around us.

"Move out," she says. "Chase, stay with me." She doesn't speak again until her Furies have gone. "You don't leave my side. The head of the Huntresses has questioned our ability to lead this search. She named you specifically as someone who should be left out tonight."

*Shiiit.* The head of the Huntresses might as well be the unspoken leader among the seven Houses, able to sway any crucial vote her way with her reputation as being considered the most knowledgeable, reasonable, and fair. If she's against me, I'll have a hard time overcoming whatever obstacles she throws in my way. "Did she say why?"

"I didn't give her a chance. While we organized the search, the way she talked about shifters? I don't know. It seemed off to me." Maizie shakes her head. "Everything went wrong tonight, so I'm probably overreacting, but let's not find out."

Ghosting behind her, I keep my mouth shut and my walk damn near silent. The other Houses act like this search is some kind of scavenger hunt, more of a show than reality. The Muses flutter from place to place as if they're hosting a mystery-themed party. The Mad Maes have set up a thirst aid station stocked with spelled wines.

"Come to work our bar?" one asks with a giggle.

They didn't see the grisly murder scenes or watch Dottie self-destruct with guilt and heartbreak.

I did.

With the Houses tromping through the staff quarters, the scents come through muddled. They've destroyed the best trails for a shifter to track. I won't let that stop me. If the killer's here, I'll find him.

The leader of the Huntresses steps into the hall, tall and imposing. "I already have the wolves and deer on the scent. Keep your pet cat leashed, Fury. Everyone knows they're sneaky beasts."

What'd I ever do to piss her off? Nothing as far as I know. Or maybe she hates all shifters the way she's talking as though we're animals to be controlled.

Maizie slides a cool look over the woman, something minor gods might not dare. "This is our hunt by right, not yours. Would you deny our immortal mothers their divine vengeance?"

Her words make me swallow a hiss and send shivers over my skin, something ancient and wild in the magic they invoke. They must work on the Huntress as well. After a few seconds of intense staring, she backs off, and we move along the hall faster than before.

"Well done," I whisper to Maizie. "I didn't know anyone outside the Syndicate received more than basic trainings on House law." Or that's the rumor spread to us grunts at The Rink.

"I don't. But my triad sisters—"

"The twins?"

She grins. "You know they're not actually twins, right?"

"Everyone treats them as though as they are." I don't add *WannaBe One and Two* as Kiva says, which seems accurate given their mutual love of prestige, expensive clothes, bottle blonde, and not much else.

"Both of them had graduate-level education before they turned Fury—one in law, the other in mythology and folklore."

"Huh, that's unexpected." I can't imagine either of them having the attention span to study.

"And valuable when you need trusted advisors to scare off a Huntress." She stops in front of a house with a retired Muse, a human male, and three kids standing outside. "We'll be as quick as we can."

The Muse tightens her grip on her children. "Just find him. Keep our babies safe and keep us coming home to them."

I check the house, finding no more than I'd expected. It goes like that for two hours. I sort through the smells and hit on House members who've been through visiting or pretending to search or whatever, but no one's actually found a clue.

"One more wing of the apartments to go." Maizie sounds as frustrated as I feel. Her scent's probably giving that off, but this place reeks of distrust, annoyance, and fatigue by now. Everyone's tired of the search. Their amped-up adrenaline's not helping as the smells jumble into a blur.

Heading to a door, I raise my hand to knock but stop. There's the almost human scent from The Rink. I've been here before, and it definitely didn't smell this way then. Either someone's visiting or someone has gotten sloppy.

"Maizie." My whisper's low enough no one else should be able to hear except a shifter, and that's definitely not a shifter I'm reading inside the apartment. "This is still Marty's place, right?" My fear wraps around that last vowel like I'm channeling Dottie's twang and begging her to contradict me. How had I missed this last time? Or had it not been there then?

The Fury's leader checks a list and nods, as though she's caught my hesitation to say anything too loud. When dealing with someone or *something* supernatural and not quite human, who knows what extra senses or skills they might possess? For example, the Furies don't smell all the way human, and we know they're scary. I know the scents of every House, every shifter species, every supernatural who has come to The Rink, and this one? This stink? It's different, yet it's the same I smelled at the locker room and at the murders of both Neda and Coach.

There's no heartbeat coming from within, but not every being has one. Just ask the House of Styx.

I meet Maizie's gaze, point inside, and reach for the knob, nice and slow. No need announcing ourselves to whatever's inside.

She brushes me aside and kicks open the door, a flaming sword in her hand. So much for subtlety.

As if she shrieked some war cry, Furies rush past me, weapons to call at the ready and the potent smack of vengeance pouring off them. I go in armed with fangs and claws, but when we get inside, we don't find anyone.

Furies clear the only four rooms and discover nothing but boring furniture and an empty, massive set of shelves that might've been used for books pre-Witching Wars. Other than those, the place has nothing—no holo-frames, no screens, no posters or art on the wall, no limited edition merch from The Rink that all employees bring home.

"It's empty." Sadie announces the obvious, staring at me like that's somehow my fault.

The smell fades away from the door. My senses tell me whatever left the scent has been inside this room, but the trail stops as though interrupted. "Something's blocking the scent."

"Like what?" Kiva asks.

They drop their weapons, and I withdraw mine. I don't understand how I got this wrong. Every Fury leaves except Dottie's triad sisters. Maybe Maizie signaled for them to stay with me when I was distracted or maybe she's quit caring about my safety since I haven't proven useful.

"I'm not saying you have any idea what you're talking about," Sadie says to me. "But where does the scent end?"

"At the doorframe." I gesture to the plain wood that's not even painted. "So unless whatever left it poofed like your immortal mother, someone used—"

"A cloaking spell." The Fury who can't stand me unfurls her wings and zooms toward my head, not stopping when I use shifter speed to get out of her way. She runs her fingers over the top of the frame as if checking for dust. "Ooh, these are old symbols."

"What's it say?" Kiva moves to join her.

"Not sure." Sadie barely dodges the other Fury's wings. "My family studied Celtic pagan ways, not ancient Greek or whatever this is. Doesn't look like any ward I know. It could be a cloaking spell, or it could be some weird call on the gods for blessing."

"What else can we look for if it's a cloaking spell?" I ask because no way could the scent be explained away by some holy graffiti.

"Something out of the ordinary." Sadie taps on her comm. "I'll see if I can find a translation."

Everything about tonight seems out of the ordinary, from Coach's murder to Connie's kidnapping to this messed-up attempt at a real investigatory search. We should've begged the marshals to come, no matter who in that office might've leaked my location to Peaches. That damage was already done with no benefits. What else could've gone wrong?

I stare at the empty shelves, wondering why Marty had something so archaic put in when no one I know owns actual books except a few of the House leaders. Tugging at a corner, I find the unit's attached to a wall. There's no wall here in my place. The realization hits me. "This apartment's layout mirrors mine."

Kiva glances my way. "Congrats?"

Sadie keeps her focus on the symbols. "You might want to talk to an interior decorator about taking out atrocities like that bookcase and coming into this century."

"Mine doesn't have one of these." I tap on the wood, testing the sounds to see if the knock goes hollow. "Something only a grunt would know, but the staff quarters didn't build one-bedroom models in this layout. There should be another bedroom instead of this."

"A hidden room?" Kiva asks with a glee that I've only heard when she talks about hurting someone.

"Maybe." I *thunk, thunk* my knuckles against the back of the shelves again.

Both Furies speed across the room as if I've found Connie, a reanimation elixir for Coach, and Zeus's lightning bolt in one crappy piece of furniture. The three of us thud and thump and drum until we find a spot where the bang sounds low and deep.

I can hear the noise echo beyond. "Here. But how do we get the thing open? There's got to be a lever or a button."

"Could be remote access," Kiva says. "No time to look. Just yank the fucker out."

Using our supernatural strength, the three of us pry the center shelves from the fake wall, leaving a gaping hole where someone boarded up the opening.

I climb into the darkness first, relying on my cat vision. "The scent's stronger here. There's no bed, but he has a desk, statues scattered across a table, real pictures on the walls. Not a holoframe in sight."

Kiva comes next, pulling a flashlight from a pocket and flicking it on. "Oh my gods, look at those pages on the wall. Are those actual newspapers? Where'd he find those old things?"

Sadie follows. "He keeps a shrine." She sounds worried, unnerved.

"Yeah, but to what?" I ask, fumbling at the rusted latches of a big trunk with wheels. No way am I leaving an obvious hiding space unopened in a secret room.

"Whoever these statues depict." Sadie shines her light over the table. "They all seem to honor the same goddess, but not one I recognize. There's an inscription—*Atë*. Ever heard of her?" I shake my head. "He has food out in tribute and—" She pinches dried pieces of plant from a bowl, sniffs, and makes a face. "Bloodroot, wolf's bane, and possibly ipecacuanha root. Why would he keep herbs to induce vomiting?"

I stop what I'm doing. "To have an alibi for Neda's murder. He must be the one who caused the food poisoning that night."

"He poisoned himself?" Kiva asks, coming toward me. "Here, let me help." Not bothering with caution, she bashes the metal latches with one of the statues.

Flinching, I wait for the worst, but nothing happens. "Guess he doesn't use traps or protection wards." Tearing off the taped seals and tossing back the lid, I immediately gag and step away. The stench of death overpowers the room.

Kiva slams the trunk shut again, covering her mouth and nose. "Now we know how he transported the dead humans. It must be spelled to block the stench, probably magicked to throw off detectors and scales too." Her words come out muffled.

Creeped out by the answers we've already uncovered, I move closer to the news printouts, something I've only ever seen on my comm or holo-screens. "The headlines talk about a serial killer executed by the humans years ago." I scan the smeared pages that've been cobbled together like an old-fashioned mural, looking for something that might be a clue. A small photo on the last sends my heart racing, my breath catching, and my cat clawing for release. Marty. He's the serial killer, alive again somehow.

"I found chains." Kiva flies to me, holding them out. They smell of blood and of Connie.

Sadie sweeps away the shrine with a crash, pulling out pinned papers from beneath the toppled statues. "He has merch photos of Dottie with her eyes crossed out." Fear tightens her voice.

"Find Maizie." I run for the balcony, yelling over my shoulder. "I'm headed for the House of Furies." Swinging over the railing, I drop from floor to floor until I hit the ground, shifting into lion as I go.

Please let me be wrong.

Let Connie be safe.

Let him be somewhere else.

Let him wait until his normal date to kill again.

Or let me get to Dottie before he does.

# 18

## DOTTIE

IN THE HOURS SINCE EVERYONE LEFT FOR THE SEARCH, I TRAIN WITH every weapon I can find in the House of Furies with the hope that this time when my cousin's life's at stake, when I've lost everyone but Connie and Chase, maybe now my weapon to call might decide to show up. I zoned out on the body armor specifications Maizie described for my fancy Fury battle gear, but right now, I'm glad the outfit moves with me and allows room for my wings.

Yes, I practice wings out because I'm still prone to flying into stuff. My freaky featherless flappers appear when I'm scared, stressed, or just freaked out, which means I've smacked my triad sisters in the face with wings more than a few times. At least mine don't have blades like Kiva's.

She explained that getting my wings caught in my weapon to call would be more than embarrassing, it could be deadly, so I'm taking extra care to keep my arms out while testing a leather contraption that looks more BDSM dungeon-appropriate than deadly. This slingshot qualifies under the ancient weapons rule —like Sadie's whip or Kiva's hatchet.

The leather and lead whir, and I zip the weapon faster in a figure-eight pattern in front of me since overhead circles would take out the tips of my wings. The pattern feels right, exact this time, and excitement shoots through me. Sadie says ancient soldiers could be lethal with the amped up child's toy.

*Maybe the slingshot is my weapon to call.*

I release the lead ball, and it shoots across the room, crashing into hanging shields opposite my target. They smash to the ground in a clatter.

*Or maybe not.*

I clean up the mess, thinking I'm right back where I was in the human world, picking up after accidents—except now, I'm the walking accident. Impatience and disappointment roll through me, giving me a headache on top of the cuts and scrapes from tonight's experiments. Checking my comm for the thousandth time, there's no missed messages. I hate being stuck here, unable to join the search or find a weapon to call or look for Connie or even leave the House of Furies. Not okay on so many levels.

A soft *thunk*, *thunk* at the door has me spinning. Chase would've messaged me, or he would come back with my sisters. The Furies wouldn't knock. They would barge in, and who the heck else would make the climb to our flight deck? Grabbing the nearest weapon because this could be how a horror show starts—stupid half-Fury all alone in the House goes to the door unarmed—I hurry and look out the peephole, but there's nothing but darkness.

"Screw off sideways," a familiar drawl says. "No one's home."

*Connie.*

I yank open the door.

Marty stands on the other side, one hand behind his back and the other holding a tiny black circle. "Hello, Dottie."

I push past him to look for my cousin.

He blocks my path. "Uh uh." The man's fast, really fast for a human, almost Fury fast, but I catch a glimpse around his slight frame.

Connie stands across the flight deck, way too close to the edge where I pushed Chase over. Or my cat pretended I'd shoved him. The light behind me shows shadows on her face, smudges that look like blood streaked with tear stains. "I'm so sorry, Dottie," she says. "About Coach. She didn't see him, not 'til too late. He ambushed us. I fought—"

"Silence," Marty snaps, blocking my view and raising the small circle. "Does your cousin never shut up?"

"What are you doing?" I try to step around him again, but he moves with me. "Connie? What's going on? Are you okay?"

He brings his other hand out from behind his back, holding a high-powered assault rifle. "Who knew neither of you could be quiet? Let me explain."

"Yeah, do that," I tell him, propping the war hammer I grabbed from the training room against my shoulder. What happened to helpful, sweet Marty? Who is this? His evil twin? "Before I use my Fury training to go through you."

"Hmm." He doesn't sound concerned. "I'd blow up your little cousin first. See, she's rigged with explosives, and this?" Raising the black circle, he traces what looks like a button. "This is the remote to those explosives."

I eye the remote, gauging whether or not I'd be fast enough to knock it from his hand.

"Don't," he warns, moving so I can see Connie. She's bound at the ankles with her hands wrenched behind her back. A gag hangs at her chin. The blood and bruises enrage me, but Marty has his finger on the trigger, his thumb on the detonator.

"She's hurting," I plead.

He aims a cold stare at me, all traces of the friendly props manager gone. "She's alive, and there's no immortal who can bring someone back if they're in pieces. I've killed you once. I won't hesitate to do it again, and this time, you'll stay dead like you were supposed to. Drop your weapon."

"Let Connie go." If I can distract him, if I can delay him until Chase or my sisters return... "She's just a kid."

"But she's someone you care about, so no, she'll be staying right where she is." He glances toward my weapon. "Put down your lovely war hammer."

I hesitate. If I let go of the hammer, I'll be unarmed and unable to help my cousin. Other than being stronger and faster with slightly accelerated healing, I'll be nothing more than a human with pretty wings. Never have I wanted my weapon to call more. "Why are you doing this, Marty?" My voice comes out small.

"Uh uh, I'm not launching into some clichéd villain monologue while you hold on to the hammer. Put. It. Down. Don't make me tell you again."

I drop the weapon and raise my hands, palms out. "All right. At least tell me why you hate supernaturals so much. I should've guessed when you looked so stunned to see me at The Rink as a Fury." To think I'd wondered if Chase had been jealous that night when I should've been suspecting the serial killer in front of me.

He laughs a cold, bitter sound. "I couldn't care less that you're a Fury. My only surprise was that you hadn't stayed dead."

"You killed Neda." My first accusation comes out strangled. "And Coach." My heart closes in a fist around the second. Connie struggles against her bindings, and I do my best to silently warn her to be still. "Why target them?"

"I needed to get the Houses' attention," he says. "Leaving dead humans dressed as deity daughters hadn't done the job. Their search started when you died, so I gave them murders connected to you, knowing your shifter would press for the investigation. With Coach's death, the Furies would be primed for a full-scale war."

"Against you?" I ask. Marty's not just psycho. No, he wants to provoke the most feared deity daughters into hunting him down.

"Of course not. They won't suspect me. With the massive

search happening at the staff quarters, the seven Houses will be pissing one another off until they're ready to tear the city apart and each other to pieces."

"They'll find you. Chase has your scent." I step closer to draw his attention because Connie's glancing over the side of the flight deck ever so slowly as if judging how many stories up we might be. I need to steal that remote from him and get her out of harm's way.

"One of my scents among many, the beauty of cloaking spells and illusions. If by some slim chance they decide I'm a suspect, they'll be looking at The Rink as it's the last place I swiped my access card before heading here. No one's coming to save you. No, I came because history told me they'd leave you here unprotected, alone." He shakes his head, curling his lip in an ugly imitation of a grin. "You're all so naïve, so convinced you know everything as the great Houses protected by the Syndicate. Well, let me tell you, I'd be running Syn City if I had been brought back as a deity daughter instead of a deity son."

Hold on. "What?" I'm shaking, and I can't catch a breath. Fear for Connie and shock at his answer has me almost gasping. "You're the son of an immortal?"

"Gods-spawned just like you," he says. "I was chosen by Atë, the trickster goddess who specializes in mischief and delusions. My mommy dearest's so wicked she got kicked out of Olympus by Zeus himself. Stirring up a little trouble for Syn City with some dead humans seemed the least I could do to prove my worth to her."

"Their lives—my life—meant nothing to you." A deep ache spirals from my chest down, down, down to the soles of my feet. If I didn't count, if Coach and Neda didn't matter, then killing Connie won't be a problem for him either.

She flicks her gaze over the dizzying drop again, her bottom lip trembling the same as it did when she fell from her first bike and scraped her knees.

I can't let him hurt her. Sorrow and desperation drown me, pulling at me like a boulder strapped to my ankles. "I'm the one you want. Please don't hurt Connie. I'll beg. I'll do anything." I keep his attention on me, on my pain and torment if that's what gets him off.

"Oh, I like you." His gaze lights up as if I've given him some sick gift. "The way you ran that night, the way you stood to fight me at the last second. You've been my *favorite*." He twists the word as if he can taste it on his tongue. "But tonight, you have nothing to bargain with."

"Shows what you know." Connie pipes up from her dangerous and deadly position, and I want to slap my hand over her mouth to keep her quiet, to make him forget she's there, but no, she's smirking her teenager screw-you rebel smile. "I'm changing her odds."

Connie jumps.

*Nooo.*

# 19

## DOTTIE

No, no, no. My world somersaults like a deranged cheerleader, spinning and twisting to donkey kick me in the face. My gut threatens to hitchhike a ride with my heart up my throat, and I can't scream, can't gasp, can't breathe. Not Connie. She has followed me around since she could toddle and trusted me to keep her safe.

I failed her.

Oh gods, how I failed her.

I dash past Marty to the edge, not wanting to see her crumpled body on the ground but not able to accept the reality otherwise. He skids next to me, his cursed deity-given speed as fast as mine. Nausea bubbles bile in a sour wash over my tongue, and tears burn my eyes. *Not Connie.* The wish beats in my head, a steady *thump, thump, thump* drumming that's all I can hear over the roar of blood in my ears. We both peer over the side.

But it's not Connie that's leaping from branch to branch with smooth, lethal grace. No, it's Chase in human form with supernatural speed and Connie in his arms.

She made it! The thought wraps around me, heady and hopeful. Chase hits the ground, feet first in a sure feline landing.

Ripping the explosives from Connie's neck, he hurls them through the woods toward the swamp. My heart soars along with the horrible bomb that the madman beside me dared to strap on my baby cousin.

"Damnit," Marty yells and raises the assault rifle into a ready-fire position.

"No." I shove into his side, knocking his shot wide and the remote from his hand. It falls over the side and spirals toward the ground. The boom of gunfire reverberates in my ears.

There's a shriek from below that's haunting, a mountain lion's yell that might as well be a deafening scream. A glance shows Chase in cat form, bigger than any cougar I've ever seen. He's massive and hunkered over Connie like he'll rip apart anyone who comes near her. Thank the gods for my shifter.

"Bitch." Marty's voice comes out a near growl, and my victory's short-lived. He backhands me—unfortunately, he's stronger than he looks—hard enough to shove me off the flight deck.

Gravity takes over, and wind rushes up to meet me. I unfurl my wings and zoom toward him, but not fast enough to keep him from firing again. The *bang* has me flinching, wrapping my wings tight around me, but there's a whizzing sound, a zipping that's close enough to ruffle my hair. Rushing to get to Marty before he can pop off another shot, a terrible yowl of pain has dread exploding in my gut and fear-soaked adrenaline flooding my system.

*Chase.*

I look over my shoulder, and he's down, sprawled in cat form partially covering Connie. Neither of them move. Oh gods, have I lost them both? My ears ring, hot tears burn my eyes, and my lungs go into lockdown. This can't be possible. How could I lose both the people I love, the only ones in the whole world, with the same shot?

Marty takes aim again, and I fly at him, pushing the rifle's barrel skyward and grabbing for the weapon, but either I miscalculate, or he's too fast, too strong. The stink of gunfire hangs in the air, and devastation drags me down even as I beat my wings harder.

"See what you made me do?" Marty screams. He whips the butt of the rifle like a club, and the hard metal and plastic smacks me in the face.

The momentum forces me away from the flight deck, and I struggle to stay upright with him hitting me again and again. For every inch I gain, he slams me a yard backward. Another vicious blow, and I can taste blood in my mouth, feel the warm trickle through my hair. Pain radiates across my senses, making me want to curl into a ball rather than take another wallop.

Why fight when I've already died once? When I didn't want to become the killer that this second life requires? When Chase and Connie may be gone? I can't face that.

They have to live.

*I* have to live. Because they'd want me to.

Resolve spins through me, stiffening my spine rather than letting me shield myself. I throw myself on the deck and roll, scrambling away from Marty and toward the tossed war hammer, not taking my gaze off him. He's done so much to destroy Syn City. I will stop him for Neda, for Coach, for Connie, for Chase. For my mate.

*My mate.*

In trying to save me, Chase had vowed a blood oath to an immortal. He'd tried to save Connie. Whether I could save him or not, I want to stay with him for as long as any bond would allow, no matter how much or how very little time we might get.

The colors I'd imagined before? The vivid hues tied to his emotions? In my mind, I can see them everywhere—a dizzying and blinding rainbow of enraged reds, violent violets, and grieving greys. Chase gave me time to decide about the mating bond, and I make my choice. I latch on to the connection, opening myself fully to allow any bond between us to flow through me with no uncertainty, no limits, no strings.

Power thrumming through the bond slams into me. It's raw and vibrant and all-consuming. Chase's primal needs for the outdoors, for speed, and for the hunt mingle with my unspoken needs to belong, to feel safe, to love and be loved. The potent blend of us together? An unstoppable force.

As I might've been if I had only embraced my new life as a Fury earlier.

"No more." My voice comes out harsh, rough like it splinters on the initials of full-fledged Furies carved into the wooden boards beneath me as I crawl across the flight deck. "No more murders. No more fear. No more you." Saying the words aloud feels like a promise, a prophecy.

Marty sneers. "I'd be scared except we both know you would've stopped me already if you were a real Fury. You're not, are you?"

No. But I will be—starting now. I dig deep within to answer the question Neda had asked me my first night here. Who would I become while I was in Syn City?

A mother friggin' Fury.

Vengeance races through my veins, and I welcome the wrath. It fills me, stripping away my doubts. This feeling, this empowerment, this need for revenge after the pain and heartache he'd caused? It'd been the gift passed on to me by the immortal, her mission for my second life. Marty's reign of horror would end now, with me. Since he knocked on the door to the House, my world has turned upside down in a matter of seconds. Now, time slows, and I can seize every moment to deliver the brutal justice of the deities. I'll strangle him with my bare hands if necessary, no weapon to call needed.

Slamming my arms out, I grab the rifle. Marty's wide eyes and slack jaw give away his surprise as much as the loosened grip on the gun. I yank it away.

He shakes his head as if waking up, then stares at me with his already annoying, so-superior-to-me scorn. "Going to use that on me?"

I consider the possibility, but Coach's warning of curses on those who fire a gun against an immortal's child have me deciding against it. No wonder he'd beat me with the butt of the rifle. He'd known better than to shoot me. No way will I risk a curse for firing at him. I might miss, or it might be out of ammo, or so many things could doom my klutzy self. "No." I toss the rifle as far as I can into the swamp, hoping it'll sink deep in the muck with the sea hags and gators.

"Interesting." He lunges for the war hammer, but I kick it away.

"Not this time." I flex my wings, letting them lift me off the flight deck and stretch my hands to steady myself. Two giant curved blades ablaze with blue flames materialize, the short metal handles cold against my palms. Marty staggers back.

Heeled boots thunk to the wood behind me. "I'll be damned," Sadie says. "She found her weapon to call."

"Heck yeah." Kiva sounds delighted. "Dottie's like the ice queen meets the grim reaper."

"The reaper carries a scythe." Sadie doesn't say the *duh*, but it's implied. "Those are big-ass sickles."

"Oh, because it doesn't have a pole thing," Kiva says, her wings zinging at the same time Sadie's rustle.

My vision sharpens to almost cat-like clarity in the darkness, focusing on Marty and nothing else. A gift from Chase? Maybe. Raising the sickles and moving forward, I force Marty to the edge of the flight deck. He can fly or fall, the same as he threatened Connie by making her stand on the brink. My Fury sisters hover a few feet in front of us. "You two going to help?" I ask.

"Dayyyum, check out your Fury eyes, all black and perfect," Kiva says. "No help needed. Go full Fury on his ass."

"Connie and Chase are below—" I swallow the lump of

nothing and every-dang-thing in my throat and press the flames closer to Marty's skin. "I don't know—"

"On it," Sadie calls, and they whoosh toward the ground.

"Ooh, got me now," Marty taunts and crouches low. "I give up. What'll you do?"

I hesitate, and my pause gives him time to pull a knife from his boot and slice at my calf. My battle gear absorbs most of the damage, but the sharp blade still stings. He stabs upward, straight for my heart. I slash both sickles with Fury speed and strength, the weapons finding their target as though wielded by a master. Or magic. The sickles take Marty's head.

"For Coach and Neda and the human women you murdered," I whisper. "For me. For Connie and Chase."

My promise to my creator is complete. My mission finished, I drop my hands to my side, and the weapons disappear. I refuse to feel guilt, to feel anything but grief over losing the people I loved before I shed my first life as a human and embraced my second.

Fast footsteps behind me have me spinning, and the sickles magic themselves back into my hands—ready to strike again if necessary.

Kiva skids to a stop, sparing the briefest glance at a beheaded Marty before appearing to forget about him. "Connie," she says breathlessly. "Chase. They're alive. Injured, bleeding, but alive. Come quick."

My heart soars. *Hope.* I run after Kiva to the edge of the flight deck and jump, knowing I've got this. With my cousin and my mate and my Fury sisters, *we've* got this.

# 20

# CHASE

LAZING IN THE SUNLIGHT WITH A FULL PITCHER OF SWEET TEA, TWO massive sandwiches loaded with all the fixings, and Dottie North curled next to me in a hammock wearing a pair of short shorts and a cropped derby shirt? It's the fantasy I never could've believed might become a reality. Yet, here we are. Almost dying to save my mate and her cousin sucked, but the pampering and spoiling I've gotten since? Every big cat's dream.

"Ready for tonight's publicity event?" I ask, knowing how much she hates the hype. "I created a special Doll Deadly cocktail to serve at your autographing debut."

"Ugh, I'll never be ready for promo crap. What am I supposed to say when I sign people's stuff? Enjoy my scrawl?" Dottie snuggles closer. "Plus, I'm not sure you should be back at work. Marty shot you." She taps me with each syllable of the last. As if I might've forgotten. I got lucky he was a crappy shot.

"Superior shifter healing powers," I say instead because I'm not missing a minute of my badass Fury mate making me out to be a hero. "How's Connie?"

"Enjoying her status as an honorary member of the Fury

family. I can't believe her dad signed off on her staying in Syn City. She almost died."

"But she didn't. She walked away with scrapes and bruises—"

"Thanks to her cougar shield. If you hadn't been there... I can't stand to think about what could've happened."

"Then don't." Because I sure as hell don't want to. "Connie's nearly sixteen."

Dottie sighs dramatically. "What does *anyone* know at sixteen?"

"I fell for you younger than that." I drop the confession into the conversation all casual to distract her from her worries for a moment.

"You did not." She sounds irritated.

Not the reaction I'd hoped for, but I'll take it. "You're cute when you're contrary."

"You're such a cat." She says the endearment like high praise. Yeah, she can't stay mad at me. "But what do I do about Connie?"

"She agreed to see the trauma counselor, right?"

"Yes, but I haven't checked the woman's credentials yet." She stiffens in my arms, her shoulders creeping toward her ears. "I meant to."

I know why she hasn't done that homework. Part of the deal with the Syndicate for Connie being allowed to stay is that she, Dottie, and I all promised to report to counseling. "The doc's great, and she's really nice. Plus, she gives off strong cat vibes, so you'll love her."

"Just because I love you doesn't mean I trust any cat to see Connie."

"True," I admit. "But the Furies have the best psychologists in the world."

"Why would a top therapist live in the swamp?"

"Your House has a bunch of murder victims living together with a mission for vengeance. Y'all deserve the best. *You* deserve the best. Which is why you have me." She snickers, and the sound lights me up like fireworks.

"Arrogant shifter."

"Awesome Fury."

"All right, I'll try to be less anxious about Connie staying, but are you sure you want the cottage that the Furies offered to loan us?"

"I've told you." But I'll tell her another fifty times if she needs to hear it to believe me. "I can't wait to move in with you, and I adore your cousin like a bratty baby sister."

"I won't tell her you called her that."

"She's tough. She can take it. Petunia women don't scare easily." When Dottie goes quiet, I worry I've said the wrong thing. With anyone else, I wouldn't care, but the cat prowls inside me. Neither of us can stand to see our mate upset. "What is it?"

"I messaged my momma today." There's a hollowness to her voice, something I haven't heard since the fight where she went full Fury.

"And?"

"She told me not to message again, that she wants the money but not me."

Anger makes my blood boil hellfire hot, and I want to curse her mom, who I've always hated, but I won't because that'd hurt Dottie. Instead, I hold my mate close, hoping she knows the rejection is rooted in her mother's issues and not her. "Her loss."

"Thanks." Sadness underscores her answer, but resignation comes through too. "I didn't tell Connie; I think she already knew. We don't need any more drama after the nightmare with Marty and...you know, how it ended."

"Don't feel bad about what you did." I'm damn proud of her, and my cat wishes he could tear into the fucker again, but that's not the reassurance she needs. "Vengeance is your gods-given mission."

"Yeah, but he came back as a deity's kid too. Maybe *he* had some weird mission."

"You didn't see the news feeds about the serial killer Marty was as a human. No god would've brought him back for any reason except chaos. He would've kept killing until someone put him down like the monster he was."

She doesn't say anything for a few minutes, but she's thinking because she's tapping my chest with her index finger in the way she does when she's puzzling through hard stuff. "Tell me something good," she says finally. "Something happy."

"My Ma's making me insane with questions about you as a Fury, wanting to know what your favorite foods and things are now so she can bring presents when she comes to visit."

"Soon, right?" Hope hooks her question at the end with one of those happy exclamation points with the hearts that she draws. "To put an end to Peaches and her plot to steal away my mate as a stud."

"I *am* a stud." I can joke now that I have my mate and I'm not in danger of being shipped off to the highest bidder. Of course, Dottie claiming me means I no longer want to kill every male who looks in her direction. Just snarling at them will suffice. "I'm the most handsome cat shifter in Syn City." The only one, but still.

"Humble, too," she says.

"Very."

"Stop bragging and tell me Peaches will be leaving town any day now."

"She will. Ma is coming to wrap up the deal with her, alpha-to-alpha so to speak, but it sounds as though Peaches has already found business alliances here and possible cougar mate connections."

"Really?" She tips her head to look up at me, propping her chin on her hands stacked on my chest. The pose is adorable and sexy and so Dottie. "How?"

"The twins."

"Maizie's WannaBe triad sisters? *Those* twins?"

"Yep. Who knew those two would be so awesome as her advisors?"

"Maizie's a pretty awesome Coach. Not the same, but..." Her voice trails off, and she looks haunted for a moment before blinking the sadness away.

Yep, we're definitely going to see the therapist given we've been through more in the last few weeks than other couples might face in a lifetime. I smooth a hand over her hair, a spark of happiness winding through me when she leans into my touch. "But we'll make the best of this world we've been given."

"What about the shifter murders and the wolf marshals?"

"What about them?"

"We don't know if that was Marty or someone else."

"I don't think Marty killed those shifters. He preferred sneak attacks, and whoever hunted the shifters had to be someone far more skilled." And evil. My stomach turns just thinking of the vicious and depraved crime scene photos. "Besides, the marshals had a snitch who gave me up to Peaches so they can deal with their own problems. Any other worries in that head of yours?"

Her hesitation means yes, but I wait for her to speak. A long stare off between us gives me more time to study how beautiful she is in the sunlight.

"Think you can be happy shacked up forever with a Fury?" she asks.

"I'm more than ready for our forever." I haul her up for a kiss, a dizzying spiral of the mating bond wrapping around us as I brush my lips against hers. That bond hitting me even harder when she teases me with her tongue. Deeper than any connection I could've hoped for, the link promises we'll always be together more than words ever could. I can't imagine life without her.

She pulls away. "Enough to marry me or whatever the deity daughter equivalent to a wedding might be?"

A pulse of pleasure thrums through our connection, and my heart threatens to leap from my chest on a wave of, *Please gods, say she wants to claim me as her mate not just to shifters who'll recognize it on scent, but to everyone.* "Did you just propose?" I can't catch a breath, and I go stalker-cat-still waiting for her answer.

Wariness flickers in her gaze, one predator recognizing another in ambush mode. "If I say I did..." The same suspicion colors her tone, slowing her speech as though she's waiting to see who will make the first move. "Would you say yes?"

"Yes. A million times yes. A friggin' billion times." Whatever it'll take to mark her as mine and me as hers for all time.

She curves her lush lips in a heartbreaking half grin. "Then, I guess I did. Let's get hitched."

Fuck yeah! "We're getting married." Joy has me damn near purring.

"Yeah, we are." She kisses me, and I swear fireworks burst through the mating bond. I want to kiss her until tonight's work at The Rink forces us apart in a few hours.

Nothing can interrupt my happiness right now. Not the sudden flutter of wings or Sadie swearing with creative aggravation or her irritation-laced scent.

"My balcony." A growl works its way up my throat. "Flap those wings off it." I don't stop kissing my Fury, who's now giggling against my mouth. The taste of her laugh? Better than anything has ever been.

"Oh yay," Kiva says. "We got here just in time to go voyeur on their make out session. I should've brought the cocaine-laced popcorn."

"How many times do I have to tell you?" Sadie rocks full grump gruffness. "There's no coke in the popcorn, and gods, you'd think they haven't sucked face the entire time since we stitched him up."

I glare at them, hoping they take the hint and go bother someone else. No such luck.

Kiva hops on the railing, leaning against a post and stretching her legs out to cross at the ankles. "You two are so smoochy cute. I want a hot kitty."

"Nope," Sadie says. "You're stuck with a bear."

Dottie whips around to stare at her sisters. "What?"

So much for kissing until those two buzz off. I might as well enjoy the sister show since these three can't talk without the conversation turning into a comedy skit better than anything put on at The Rink.

Kiva's shaking her head and making a swiping *kill it* motion toward her throat.

So, of course, Sadie doesn't stop. "A bear shifter has shown up in Syn City, and he brought Kiva a giant bag of seafood-flavored potato chips and a flat-tasting soda. To deliver that nastiness, he tried to break into the House of Furies last night."

"Nooo." Dottie sounds shocked. Understandable when most people would meet a gruesome punishment for daring to invade the House. "Please tell me you didn't throw your hatchet at him."

Kiva scowls. "As if I'd need to summon my weapon to call to run off a pesky were-bear."

"I wouldn't call him that to his face," I tell her. "They're sticklers about being teased except by family, packs, and mates."

"Whatever," Kiva says. "Who knew crab chips might be my favorite snack? I've never tried them before. Not in this life anyway, but who knows—"

I interrupt her. "A shifter brought you food and you ate it?"

She shoots me a *duh* look. "Yeah."

"That's how we initiate the mating dance," I tell her. "Every supernatural knows that."

"You sneaky cat." Dottie pokes my bicep, and I flex instinctively. "I didn't know that when you brought me cupcakes and candy."

I'm not apologizing for wooing my woman. "You were new to our world."

"And if I'd known?" Dottie asks.

"I would've still brought them."

She sends me an *I'll-get-you-later look* and glances at Kiva. "What are you going to do about your bear shifter suitor?"

"Absolutely nothing." Kiva frowns. "I need to focus on my skating. The Huntresses have a new blocking formation that I have to figure out how to take down."

"Aww." Sadie shoves at Kiva's sneaker-clad feet hard enough that Kiva has to fan her wings to stay perched on the railing. "You'll break his heart. Don't you love your wittle were-bear?"

"He's not *my* were-bear, and he's not little. The guy's massive. Not my type." She wrinkles her nose. "You can have him."

Sadie glares at her. "No way would I date a shifter. No offense, Chase."

"None taken." I'm not sure anyone bothers to listen to my answer.

"Did you two have a reason for dropping by?" Dottie asks them, climbing out of the hammock while holding my hand as if she needs to steady herself. Like she doesn't have wings and Fury strength to do that. "Other than celebrating our engagement?"

"You're getting married?" Sadie asks at the same time Kiva shrieks at a deafeningly high octave.

"Yes." Dottie's all smiles and happiness. I want to kiss the sweetness off her lips, but this is her time to celebrate with her sisters. I will have a lifetime of kisses.

"Bachelorette party," Kiva yells. "Let's head to The Rink and get the drinking started."

"That happens closer to the wedding," Sadie says. "And we're already late for Maizie's meeting."

"Drunk roller derby could totally be a thing." Kiva's not giving up her party ideas. "Let's go tell the House. It'll be epic! Holy

Hades, Chase, you scored a marriage with our triad sister. How could you be so lucky?"

Sadie almost smiles. "He made all the right moves like bargaining with an immortal and saving her life."

Kiva's bouncing giddiness is infectious. "Oh my gods, you could write a guidebook on How to Date a Fury."

I wink. "I'll send the first copy to your bear shifter."

"Shush." Dottie kisses me. "See you tonight after The Rink closes?"

"And every night after." Because her sisters are right—I've found forever with a Fury, and I can't wait to get started on our happily ever after.

Thank you for reading! Did you enjoy? Please add your review because nothing helps an author more and encourages readers to take a chance on a book than a review.

And don't miss the next book of the Syn City Shifters, FOR WHOM THE FURY ROLLS, available now. Turn the page for a sneak peek!

Also be sure to sign up for the City Owl Press newsletter to receive notice of all book releases!

# SNEAK PEEK OF FOR WHOM THE FURY ROLLS

Seven proposals, six rejections, and one *thank the gods she finally said yes* later, I can't deny my fated mate anything, even something so dangerous as leading this rescue mission for a runaway cub.

The winter wind stings my eyes and burns my nose. If I'm chilled, my human wife must be freezing. Dead branches snap under our feet, followed by the rustling of nearby wildlife curious about the predators in their midst. Beneath the creak of swaying, barren trees, the swift footfalls of other searchers scatter as they move in opposite directions.

My wife put a search team together in mere minutes. While I'm my alpha's lieutenant, I lead with thought and careful planning. Kiva's the spontaneous motivator. I'm damn proud of her ability to inspire, but wariness gnaws at me like a vicious inner monster. A smoky earthiness fills my senses, the only scent other than my mate's sexy sweetness.

Her flashlight blinks out again. Electricity has been spotty all week, and the damn thing's batteries probably only had a half charge to begin with. I can handle the transition, but she must be totally blind. The moon's a sliver in the sky. Its faint light reflected in the snow seems more shadow than brightness.

"Want me to take point?" I ask her yet again.

"No, I've got this," she says. "There's probably an emergency glow stick in the pack. I could check if my big strong bear hadn't insisted on carrying everything."

"It's our first wedding anniversary. The least I could do was offer to lug around the medic kit." That I hope we won't need.

"I know you didn't want me coming along." She speaks the truth. "But the kid's gotta be terrified."

"Or Rylie's a rebellious teenager who has outsmarted us. She probably shifted hours ago and snuggled up with wild bears in a warm cave somewhere."

"She's fifteen and crying over her crush being an idiot to her. Stupid bear shifter male."

I don't respond because arguing that point with my mate would make me one of said stupid bear shifter males. At least the rest of the search team is far enough back that we don't have an open debate of the issue. Making light of our runaway's situation doesn't help release the pressure valve on my worry about her, about Kiva, about all of us right now.

"We'll find her," my wife says. "Rylie's close. I can feel it."

My senses don't pick up any trail, not the slightest scent or sound to confirm my mate's instinct, but if she says the kid's near, I trust her to know the truth. My Kiva doesn't talk about being witch-born, mage-born, or whatever those who came into this world with magic in their blood call themselves these days. Her human half makes her an outcast to their kind, but she has an instinct that's infallible if she doesn't let doubts get in the way. "The lake's less than a quarter mile ahead. We can regroup there."

"Hate the water." Her muttered gruffness doesn't hide her fear, not from me.

Reaching for her gloved hand, I squeeze when she links her fingers through mine. "Me too." I don't have Kiva's brutal past that she doesn't talk about, but nightmares of drowning have haunted me from childhood.

"We'll find Rylie," she says, "and we'll all go home to a nice fire."

"We will." Silence surrounds us like a thick wool blanket, but

I don't miss the chattering of Kiva's teeth. Despite supply issues, she wears the best in winter gear that we can find over her skintight jeans and a She-Devils jersey for her hockey league. But she's shivering. I should've insisted she stay behind or wear another layer or...

"Stop worrying," she says. "I can practically hear you making a list of worst-case scenarios and fixes for them."

"It's my job as your mate to protect you, provide for you even though—"

"I can do it myself."

I grin at the truth. A trained fighter with a sharp wit and sharper tongue, no one is tougher than my wife. "True, but I like taking care of you. It's why I have dinner waiting at home for our anniversary celebration."

"You only remember because I wrote it on the cabinet door, right over your favorite honey taffy."

"No, I remembered first. You slapped the note up after asking me why you shouldn't schedule a hockey practice for tonight, and you put the date there because you'd see it when going for your stash of crab chips." Yuck. Why my woman loves to ruin good potato chips with crab cake seasoning, I'll never understand. Must be a Jersey thing. "I'd already wrapped your gift before your note went up."

"You got me a present? What is it?" Her enthusiasm and refusal to focus on anything I might've said other than gift makes me laugh.

"You'll have to wait and see."

"New skates?" Happiness threads through our mating bond, as radiant and warm as Kiva herself. "They are, aren't they?"

Her single-minded devotion to her sport despite spending half of every game in the penalty box might be one of the many reasons I fell hard for her. "You think I'd give you skates for our anniversary? To celebrate finally getting you to marry me after I proposed seven times?"

"I'm picky. Even my team says that about me."

Her teammates call her prickly, but I'm not going to argue semantics. "You can be picky as long as you're mine." I kiss her cheek.

Twisting so that our lips meet, she licks at me with the tip of her tongue. "Let's find Rylie and get home so I can get my present. I'll protect you out here in the woods, my big were-bear."

"I'll let the *were-bear* insult slide this time if you let me lead until we get to the lake." Where the light might be better.

"Fine." She hands me the dead flashlight. "I should get my pick of your latest creations for my anniversary."

I'm ridiculously happy that she wants something from my forge. My blades bring in top dollar, a benefit to our entire den since who knows when the next battle between supernaturals and humans will leave us scrambling for yet another new normal.

Had the modern world seen a fighter like Kiva before magic was outed? One who relied on steel and iron and silver rather than guns? Maybe. Maybe not. We shifters rely on fangs and teeth, and the uppity magic-slingers who fought the Witching Wars a half century ago retreated to their sanctuary cities, leaving the rest of us to struggle for survival in the combat still happening around the globe. To fight things that can't be killed by technology or weapons from the past few centuries. To be what Kiva was raised to become, a hunter of the gods-spawned. She doesn't do that anymore. Not since she said yes to *us*.

"The pretty hatchet you finished last week will be mine," she says.

"We'll see." I force as much doubt as I can into my voice. The hatchet's wrapped and hidden at home. My woman loves her weapons. I got her to finally agree to my proposal with a dagger that has our intertwined initials hidden in the intricate engraving, the one strapped to her thigh now. "Almost to the lake. You want me to radio the rest of the crew?" Here's hoping the batteries in the comms held more of a charge than the defunct flashlight.

"Not yet." She edges close to the lake that's now a frozen sheet of ice. The moon's rays fall brighter here, making the ice shine like broken glass. "Do you hear something?"

"You don't have to tell me my stomach's growling. Every shifter in a mile radius knows it." The steak dinner I'd planned sounds really good right now.

She smacks my gut as if that'll make the hunger stop. "I could've sworn someone called my name."

A trickle of fear snakes its way up my spine to the base of my skull where a pounding ache kicks in. "No. I would've heard that." My senses go on full alert. "Grab the shotgun strapped to the pack."

She curves her mouth into a wicked grin. "Mmm, dirty talk from my grizzly. Someone's getting lucky tonight."

"Promise?" I ask, pretending I'm not panicking about the voice she thinks she heard. Every one of those times I proposed? Worth it for all the nights coming for the rest of our lives. "I know all kinds of ways to warm you up."

"Yeah you do." She steps away from me, studying the ground. "Hey, fresh tracks leading toward the lake." She puts her boot next to the smaller print in the snow. "Rylie went this way."

I take a deep breath. "I can't smell her, and the tracks don't look like her sneakers. You sure those are hers?"

Kiva bristles worse than any housecat, and the scent of annoyance rolls off her. "They're fresh. I've got snowflakes stuck in my lashes, and we've had at least another inch tonight. Who else would've come this way?" She yells the girl's name.

Dread has my bear rising within me, ready to shift and defend our mate, and I want to snatch back Kiva's voice from booming over the frozen expanse. "We need to get back to the den. Now."

"But Rylie—"

"Whoever's been hunting shifters these past few years? They're still out there." The few detailed reports we've gotten say the killer rips dead shifters apart in a way no human could manage. But who knows the reality? News usually favors whatever group reports it. The witch sanctuary hours south of here doesn't care about us, and to many humans, the only good shifter is a dead shifter. "Rylie's smart. She's probably already back at the den."

"Their last murder happened months ago all the way across country. Whoever's killing East Coast shifters wouldn't risk the Sierra Nevada mountains in the winter. Besides, the marshal's office said—"

"I'm not trusting any damn wolves with my mate's safety."

She opens her mouth to argue but closes it just as quickly and cocks her head toward the lake. "You had to hear her calling that time."

"That voice?" The one sending giant warnings screaming along my spine? It's wrong, magical and singsong. "That doesn't sound like Rylie."

"She's out there across the lake. I'm going after her."

"No way you're walking on that ice. We'll go around." Or I'll toss her over my shoulder and run as far as I can get her from that voice.

"This high up? It'll hold." She hurries onto the ice. I grab for her, and she dodges my grip.

"Come back, sweetheart." While I love my mate's boldness and courage, in this moment, I need her to be impulsive somewhere far away from whatever's out there. "The ice can't be more than an inch or two thick this early in the season. It's not solid enough for Rylie to cross. Or you."

Keeping my big bear body on land and not chancing the ice giving beneath my heavy weight, I reach for her, and she dashes past my fingertips, farther onto the ice. "No ocean water," she whispers. "Can't be sea witches here." Her mumbling makes no sense.

The creepy call dances across the lake again. Saltwater scents wash over me as if we've traveled to a distant ocean and not a still, freshwater lake.

"Wait." I go after her, and the ice cracks under my weight with a loud pop. "Shit."

"I'm coming, Rylie." My mate glances over her shoulder at me. "I'll be right back to you. Promise."

"Kiva, love, that's not Rylie." I don't know what the hell the voice could be, but I don't want it anywhere near my wife. Unfastening the pack, I heft it off my shoulders and to the ground.

"No. Rylie! Oh gods." Kiva takes off at a sprint.

Something whizzes across the lake, a zipping noise that echoes with a zing. Kiva stops with a jerk and spins to face me.

Fear and pain punch through our mating bond. My pulse thunders in my ears, my lungs stop working, and my vision narrows in a dizzying darkness to getting to my wife.

"Kiva?" I don't have the oxygen for a yell, don't have the grace not to scramble and slip as I rush to her. A silver-tipped arrow coated in blood gleams on the ice, the spray of vivid red leading to my wife. Her legs buckle, and she crumbles, her head thudding against the frozen hardness.

My link with Kiva—the vibrant warmth I've known since the first time I saw her—it's fading beat by slowing heartbeat. I can't breathe, can't think.

"Hold on, love." I rush to her until a loud crack beneath me sounds like a gunshot. I'm too heavy. I'll bring us both down. Dropping to my hands and knees, I crawl inch by agonizing blood-smeared inch to her.

She doesn't answer, doesn't whimper, doesn't tell me to stop being such a scaredy were-bear like she has a million times since we first kissed. I'm losing her in a fight I can't win, one I didn't even see coming. The ice groans loud and long, a fracture ready to tear us apart forever.

Farther out, a butchered and broken body sprawls as though dropped there like a gruesome gift. A bright red sneaker lies closer to us. *Rylie*. It has to be Rylie. Dear gods. I can't hear the heavy thud of her bear shifter heart or feel the hum of pack connection. Pushing down panic, I strategize. I'll save my wounded mate first and then crawl back out for Rylie.

Going down to my belly, I pull myself to Kiva. Blood rushes out of her so fast, a river I can't hold back. "Hang on, love." There's no healer or apprentice for miles. I drag her oh-so-slowly off the ice, never stopping my pleading.

Her heart goes silent.

"Don't leave me." The instant we hit solid ground again, I drop to my knees with her in my arms, the need to do anything but hold her leaving me in a rush. "Just stay with me."

I could call to the others, but they wouldn't get here in time. Not for anything but to watch the end of us.

"Please, please, please," I beg her, beg the gods, beg anyone who might listen, but the only answer comes from deep within.

Kiva's death hits like a boulder being dropped on me, the mating bond going still and silent, a void where there'd been so much life before. "No." My roar shakes the ground, thunders through the trees, and sends birds flapping away. The flapping comes so loud I can hear it over the deafening boom of blood in my ears.

I glance up at the dark night that stretches endlessly with only the ice's glare cutting into the abyss. A cloaked figure wreathed in black blinks to existence in front of us. "Are you Death? Have you come for her?" My words come out thick around the sob stuck in my throat. "Take me instead. Or let me come with her? Please?"

"You called me here with a *please*, so I've come." A woman's voice—one full of venom and fury—comes from inside the black hood. "She's a fighter?"

"Yes."

"She was your mate? The one you swore to protect with your life?"

The truth in her judgment lashes through me. "Yes." I failed to save my Kiva.

"What price are you willing to pay?" The coldness in her tone matches the shivers racking my body. Her scent isn't human, isn't shifter, isn't anything I've smelled before. "To give her another chance at life, what would you give?"

"Anything." I flinch when Kiva's head lolls to the side. "Everything." My voice cracks around the word.

"Then it's done," the woman says.

Kiva vanishes from my arms.

I scramble to grab at empty air. "Where'd she go? What've you done to her?"

"She's alive and well and far from here with no memory of this life."

My heart hooks on her last words, floundering like a fish speared. "Will she remember me? She's my mate. We're fated to be together."

"Perhaps your mating bond stopped with her death. She's beginning a new life, one where she'll have the chance to choose again if she wants a mate—whether that's you or someone else."

"I'll find her." I will. No matter how long it takes me.

"You cannot interfere with her new life."

"She needs me like I need her."

"What *you* need is not my concern. She had a brutal start to this life, and I won't burden her with such horrific memories to weigh down her next." She pauses as if thinking through possibilities. "*If* you find her, you're forbidden to speak to her of this life until you've convinced her to fall in love with you again."

"I can't tell her anything?" It took me forever to convince my mate of our destined bond the first time. Those six proposals and rejections play in a repeat loop in my mind. Sure, she'd said yes in the end, but each *no* had been devastating in its own way.

"Nothing of this life. Nor can you have someone else tell her. Until—what's it your sanitized fairy tales speak of?" She sneers.

"True love's kiss? Unless or until she falls in love with you again, she must remember on her own or not at all. It's the price for her second chance. You did say you'd pay anything."

But to give up love? Her memories of the life we'd made together? "She prefers to be called Kiva. Will you at least let her keep her name?"

"Perhaps." Her tone screams no, and I scramble for any hope to clutch in the wake of this horror.

The calls of the other rescuers who must've heard my pained roar come closer. My gut instinct screams I'm running out of precious time to find out anything about what has happened to my mate. "Can you tell me where to look for her? What kind of life you're giving her?" *Please, please be a good one.*

"I've no answers for you, only questions. Is pursuing her in her new life worth the risk of her rejecting you forever?" The woman disappears, not waiting for my answer.

Kiva's worth everything. I'll find her, and I'll win her back. I'll bring her home, and I'll never let her go again.

Don't stop now. Keep reading with your copy of FOR WHOM THE FURY ROLLS available now.

And sign up for the latest news, giveaways, and more from Luna Joya: lunajoya.com/newsletter/

Don't miss more of *Syn City Shifters* series with book two, FOR WHOM THE FURY ROLLS, available now, and be sure to sign-up to receive all the news and updates at lunajoya.com/newsletter/

**We're fated mates with a love so strong that I refuse to let death keep us apart.**

When my mate Kiva died, I bargained away everything to a mysterious supernatural. She brought my mate back to life with a curse that would forbid her to remember me, to remember *us*. The spell can only be broken by true love's kiss. Not the easiest task when it took me seven proposals to convince my fated mate to say yes the first time.

Two years later, I find her living as the mortal daughter of the mythological Furies. An amnesiac, Kiva doesn't remember me, my bear shifter clan, or how she died, but I'm here to remind her no matter what it takes.

Except someone in Syn City is out to end her life permanently and steal her away from me forever. No way am I letting that happen.

Please sign up for the City Owl Press newsletter for chances to win special subscriber-only contests and giveaways as well as receiving information on upcoming releases and special excerpts.

All reviews are **welcome** and **appreciated**. Please consider leaving one on your favorite social media and book buying sites.

For books in the world of romance and speculative fiction that embody Innovation, Creativity, and Affordability, check out City Owl Press at www.cityowlpress.com.

# ACKNOWLEDGMENTS

For those readers who told me the books had cost you a night's sleep, or you wanted to be adopted into these magical families, or you couldn't wait for the next book—this is for you. Thanks so much to every reader who spends time in my story world.

Thanks to Lisa Green for being such a supportive editor and to the entire Mystic Owl and City Owl teams. To the Paranormal Romance Rock Stars on Facebook, I couldn't ask for a better squad. To the members of Luna's Lovelies, I adore y'all.

A heartfelt thanks Lily who loves my broken heroes and Summer for being my romance fangirl bestie. To Becca Nation and Susan, y'all rock. To Lisa and Babette, thanks for being my sisters while I plot to take over imaginary story worlds. To Margie and company, I appreciate all the support and smarts. To Laura the Literary Vixen and Echo, what would I do without you?

A big kiss to my husband. You and Tiny Editor are my world. Love to my parents for encouraging imagination and wonder.

To the Bookstagrammers, reviewers, bloggers, book communities, artists, and readers who have spread the word about my witches, thank you for everything. You keep me inspired.

# ABOUT THE AUTHOR

Award-winning author Luna Joya writes steamy witch romances with mysteries, strong heroines, and the heroes who love them.

Fluent in sarcasm and penal code, Luna prosecutes crimes by day and writes at night. A survivor of traumatic brain injury with steel body parts, she lives in SoCal with her combat veteran husband and their two-pound terror of a rescue pup.

Want to be the first to get a look at covers, sneak peeks, and more? Sign up for my newsletter. Lunajoya.com/newsletter/

www.lunajoya.com

facebook.com/lunajoyawriter
x.com/lunajoyawriter
instagram.com/lunajoyawriter
pinterest.com/lunajoyawriter
bookbub.com/authors/luna-joya

## ABOUT THE PUBLISHER

City Owl Press is a cutting edge indie publishing company, bringing the world of romance and speculative fiction to discerning readers.

Escape Your World. Get Lost in Ours!

www.cityowlpress.com

facebook.com/YourCityOwlPress
x.com/cityowlpress
instagram.com/cityowlbooks
pinterest.com/cityowlpress